SOLD INTO SLAVERY

It was unthinkable that innocent Eve Doremus of Boston would be forced to parade her naked beauty in a Barbary Coast slave mart. Or that the blond giant who guarded the Sultan's female chattels would be a U.S. Marine lieutenant. Yet anything was possible in exotic, violent, 19th Century Tripoli.

Amid the love-making, intrigues and tortures of the Pasha's pagan court, Eve and her marine—Stephen Fletcher—fell in love. But their romance was destined to face every temptation and peril as they loved and battled their way to freedom.

A NOTE ABOUT THE AUTHOR

Kevin Matthews is a pseudonym for Gardner F. Fox who was born in Brooklyn and attended St. John's Prep, College and Law School. He lived most of his life on Long Island but after he married he moved to Westchester and is now living in Yonkers with his wife and two children.

He likes sports of all kinds and among his hobbies are the study of history, archaeology and the writing of amateur theatricals. His previous books include: BORGIA BLADE and MADAME BUCCANEER.

AN HISTORICAL NOVEL

BARBARY SLAVE

GARDNER FOX WRITING AS

KEVIN MATTHEWS

WILDSIDE PRESS

CHAPTER 1

The late afternoon sun made a white splendor of the city that lay sprawled across the low, sloping sands of the African coast. From the towering castle walls to the hook of the molehead that held the blue waters of its harbor, Tripoli brooded in sullen apathy at the lone frigate ship that slid through the Mediterranean like a hungry wolf pacing at the outskirts of a camp. Sunlight tipped the muzzles of its starboard cannon and put a glaze on its freshly painted deckboards. A wind whipped at the striped flag taut from its mainmast, occasionally showing the fifteen stars on its blue field.

Inside the city, men stared at the ship with venom in their eyes. Guards paced the thick white walls of the palace nestling at the northern corner of the Street of Arcades, their faces dark and gloomy. Along the stretch of sand before these walls, men in linen loincloths paused from their tasks of twisting strips of hemp to mutter oaths to Allah, as a glance showed them the big frigate prowling just outside gunnery range.

Men hated and men starved inside the city of Tripoli in this year 1805, that the Moslems called 1221. The high white walls of the Caramanli castello, that joined the sea walls to run in a height of stone as far as the Maltese castle near the mole, had been built to keep enemies out. Now these walls kept the true believers in, and those upstart Americans, who flew their stars and stripes with such unbelievable defiance, added their weight of sail and metal to act the part of jailers.

Where the Street of Arcades made a bend before the stalls of the rug sellers, a white man with only a piece of rag at his middle stirred restlessly. His eyes were feverishly bright in the dark bronze of his face as they scanned the passersby. Hunger was an ache in this man. It hurt, deep inside him,

5

and the hurt was strong enough so that he was on the point of madness.

The man moved suddenly, scurrying out of the archway as a frightened rat scurries, his eyes intent on the orange peel tossed so carelessly aside by a passing *dowedee* with his fishnets dangling over a shoulder. There was street dirt on that bit of rind, and dry dust. But to the starving man whose bony hand clawed out at it, it seemed a rare, exotic fruit.

He caught it up and slithered sideways into the shelter of a canopy overhanging the street from the doorway of a glassware stall. Nervously his fingertips went over the skin, knowing it to be big and still juicy: possibly torn off an orange from Jefren. When he was partially hidden by the striped overhang, he hunkered down and licked at the peel, his eyes closing almost in ecstasy at the bittersweet taste. He took a bite, carefully, muscles tensed against the need to wolf down this food. He chewed slowly, gently.

The starving man knew that the passersby were regarding him with amused scorn, but he was past pride. An empty belly screamed up to him that pride is an expensive luxury, and for a man who was now only a slave to the stone merchant, Ali ben Sidi of Tripoli, it ill behoved him to be spending something he did not have. And so he crouched and mouthed at his orange peel, ignoring the eyes of a slave seller whose lips were twisted in disgust, not seeing the scornful glance that a haughty corsair captain flung him as he picked his way between the street hawkers.

Voices touched his ears, but he did not hear the words.

"The nasrany is worse than an alley cur. A dog would turn up his nose at such fare."

"May Allah be blessed that I am not in his place!"

"*Inshallah!* He reminds me of the pigs I keep to eat my garbage!"

When the peeling was gone, and even as his stomach rumbled gratefully, the man stood up into the late sunlight that came over the rooftops of Tripoli to bathe his broad shoulders and deep chest in crimson light. Soon now, it would be the hour of prayer, when the muezzins would step onto the circular platforms of the mosques and call on all true believers to face toward Mecca and kneel atop their prayer mats. He was tall, this man, lean to emaciation, and there was pride in his fleshless face from which the gray

6

eyes blazed like crystals. The dirty rag at his hips was in danger of sliding from his narrow loins. A tousle of pale yellow hair, like a mop upended and thrust upon his poll, gathered the sunbeams with a reddish glint.

He moved onto the cobblestones, his eyes darting toward the gutters and beyond them into the dark mysteries of the stall shops, hoping against hope that some Turk or Arab fool had thrown away another precious bit of orange skin. The man went on more slowly. There was other food here. There had to be! He was late now, at the stone quarries. There would be lashes on his back from the black bullhide whip that fat sheriff wielded so efficiently, but he would take those lashes in exchange for one more peeling from a Tunisian orange. Stubbornly, he told himself he would not return to the quarry where they made him lug gray stones from sunrise to sunset, until he did find it.

He saw the fruit lying close by the white wall of a goldsmith shop.

It was an overripe melon, squishy and half rotten.

The man whimpered deep in his throat and ran for it. His hand was stretching downward for the big fruit when a fat man moved out of the doorway of the goldsmith shop and came forward with a quick stride. His booted foot lifted in a kick. The kick caught the starving man at the side of his face and toppled him back into the dust of the cobbled street.

He lay there on an elbow and a thigh, staring wildly up at the man who had kicked him. He saw the fleshy brown chest and black spade beard, the scimitar dangling from the belt that banded his middle, the loose green trousers that, except for the yellow boots on his feet, was his sole garment.

The starving man had been in Tripoli long enough to know this blubbery monster for a Caramanli palace guard. A member of the pasha's family was in the stall shop, buying precious ornaments. The guard threw back his head and roared vicious laughter into the warm African sunlight.

"No," said the starving man through cracked lips. "By God! No!"

He saw that Moroccan leather boot lift and poise itself above the overripe melon. Then that foot was coming down on the fruit, mashing it, making its skin burst wide apart and shower juice and pulp across half the street.

The guard laughed louder than before.

"American filth! There goes your meal! Come! Lick your food off my slipper! Eh? Here!"

The guard lifted his yellow boot with the fruit still clinging to the leather and extended it toward the man in the street.

That was when the starving man went mad.

He came off thigh and elbow in a fluid twist. His right foot took its purchase from a rounded cobblestone, and launched him in an arching leap at the hilarious guard. His big hands, like bony claws, wrapped about that taunting foot and twisted.

The guard roared his pain and his surprise. His fat body went backward, off balance. He fell heavily, directly in the arched doorway of the goldsmith shop.

The starving man went after him. The sight of that scimitar hanging in its belt chains had put a frenzy in his blood. His hand came down about its braided hilt. With an oath on his parched lips, he tugged it free. The blue steel came out into the sunlight and went yellow as the sunbeams caught it.

"Now, you Tripolitan pig, get on your feet!"

The guard lay back on both elbows and shouted. "Sa'ad! Jibran! To me! Out here in front of the shop!"

The crowd in the street paused to stare. There was a stirring among them. This naked wildman with a bared blade in his hand was a sight that struck to their hearts. A voice or two called for someone to break the neck of this crazed infidel.

The blue blade moved, and the voices fell still.

Stephen Fletcher felt the pride stir in him, driving out the anger and the madness. Not in a year and a half had he felt like this, with a weapon in his hand and his enemies ringing him in. That long ago, the U. S. frigate *Philadelphia* had run aground on the rocks east of Tripoli. He had been wearing the uniform of a marine lieutenant on that October day.

The *Philadelphia* had hit the rocks while chasing a Tripolitan corsair. Fletcher could still feel the grating crunch underfoot. Remembering what had happened then made the sweat come out on his face. They had worked hard to free it, with Captain William Bainbridge shouting orders, with the creak of davit ropes lowering a stern boat interrupting his voice, with sailors overhead loosing the topgallant sails. They were caught fast, and the Barbary pirates knew it. They came flocking in their little feluccas and barquentines, pounding the big frigate while American axes chipped away at the foremast. The foremast fell, taking the main topgallant mast with it. Guns were thrown overboard to lighten the ship forward.

As if sensing the helplessness of the big frigate, the Tripolitan gunboats swarmed in with their sakers blasting. They shot away the masts, but spared the hull. This was a prize that the corsairs would not duplicate soon again. Besides, by sparing the hull, they spared the lives of the crew, and healthy Americans would bring good prices in the slave market.

Stephen Fletcher grinned mirthlessly, remembering those hectic moments when the pirates had come aboard, fighting and wrestling with the Americans. There had been steel bared, and fists flashed here and there, as proud men sought to go down fighting. In all that wild tumult one face stood out: a hawk face, as brown as old leather, twisted into a mask of berserk rage and hate, with a small black beard below sullen, full lips and a straight, thin nose. A topknot hung like a horsetail from that shaven head, making the face seem even more sinister. Dark eyes, lighted with inner fires, bright with triumph, fastened on him and on the other marines who fought at his side. Fletcher knew the man for a reis, a sea captain, as he came swinging down on a rope hastily flung above a yardarm, his curving scimitar in a brown fist.

Fletcher had gone to meet his steel with his own service sword. Their blades had clanged twice in thrust and parry before the corsairs had swept into them and whirled them apart. But even now, all these months later, he could still see that face, in a contorted spasm of hate, and the overbright eyes glittering with triumph.

The fight had been a short one. To save his men, Captain William Bainbridge surrendered his sword to the dark man with the feverish eyes. Mustafa reis, his own men called him, with something of fright in their voices.

Most of the prisoners were to be taken before the pasha. They would be housed in the castle dungeons and held for ransom or for a prisoner exchange. There were some chosen for a different fate. Mustafa reis did the choosing. He went striding across the deck planks of the big frigate, his eyes

9

touching the faces of the sullen prisoners. Some he pointed at, and as he pointed, corsairs came and hurried these men away.

When Mustafa reis came to Stephen Fletcher, he barked something in the coast dialect and let his eyes rest on the big marine. Fletcher saw death for him in those eyes and in the hard brown contours of that face. Whatever it was the corsair captain had barked to the half-naked men at his back, the American knew it would not be a pleasant thing. Within two hours he was at the slave market. Next morning he had been sold to Ali ben Sidi, the stone merchant. For a year and a half, he had been working in the quarries, breathing stone dust and eating rotten garbage that cost his master nothing.

Now he had a chance to fight his enemies like a man. There was no broken deck under his feet, no officer roaring a command at him to lay down his arms.

He moved the curving blue blade again, and his laughter was hard and cold.

"Take it away from me! Take it—if you can!"

The crowd fell back a little, and now Fletcher saw that men were coming from the goldsmith's doorway, guards who wore the same royal green colors of the man who lay at his feet, still shouting.

A big man followed the guards out into the street. He wore a gold brocade barracan trimmed in black fur, and pointed slippers of red Cordovan leather. There was arrogance in the tilt of his chin, and in the glowing eyes that stared at the naked infidel. The brown hairs of his tiny beard quivered as he felt the defiant mockery of the American slave.

Yussuf Caramanli was the pasha of Tripoli. His thin, lightly sneering lips and bright eyes betrayed the pride that had fed on a century of power here in this coastal city. In 1714 his ancestor Mamet had come into power by murdering the Turkish soldiers who served Ahmed III. The Caramanlis had held tight to their power, using murder and treachery as their allies. When Hamet, Yussuf's brother, had come to power some years before, it was Yussuf who deposed him and assumed the throne.

Now all Europe paid him tribute. Even Napoleon Bonaparte, at whose frown the Continent shook in fear, sent him gold. London gold and Italian silver, Greek jewels and Ger-

10

man monies, all came flowing into his great, brassbound coffers. The world acknowledged the sea might of Yussuf Caramanli and paid him gold and silver and jewels for his personal enrichment, to keep his slim corsair ships from their coastal waters and his gundeck cannon from their heavily laden merchant ships.

All the world paid tribute, except for a young nation on the other side of the Atlantic Ocean. A nation of revolutionists, who had won their freedom from England only a quarter of a century ago. One of those Americans stood here before him now, with a naked sword in his hand.

Yussuf Caramanli smiled thinly. His dark hand twisted on the gold braid of the daggerhilt whose scabbard he wore, like all Moslems, in the brocaded silk sash at his middle. He spoke quickly to the man crumpled at his feet.

"What happened, Kefas? Why do you grovel like a dog before this nasrany?"

"He assaulted me, highness. Knocked me down and stole my steel!"

The starving man had never seen Yussuf Caramanli. He said boldly, "I was reaching for that melon. He kicked me and put his foot on it."

The pasha grimaced in disgust. By the black stone! These unbelievers had no pride at all! He said harshly, "Get up, Kefas! Sa'ad, give him your blade. I want this man cut in little pieces. Slowly, Kefas!"

The heavyset guard grinned and took the blade his fellow handed him. On feet that were astonishingly light for a man of his bulk, he moved toward the infidel. The starving man did not wait for him. His scimitar went high and came curving down in a molinello for the head that altered swiftly into a slanting cut at the ribs. Only for the fact that the attacking man's bare foot slipped on the pulp of the ruined melon, Kefas the Fat would have lost half his side. As it was, he got his own blade up just in time. The keen edge of the scimitar scratched his arm into red wetness, then fell away.

Steel clashed as those blued blades fell and lifted. The naked man slid and crouched, and the madness in him gave his starved muscles strength. He used the molinelli in prime and tierce until the steel seemed to blur. The bright eyes of Yussuf Caramanli followed every play of that scimitar with understanding and a little envy.

11

The fight did not last long. To the slice at the fat man's arm, the starved man added a gash at the blubbery flesh of his naked side, and a gaping cut in the hairy thigh. As those wounds dripped red blood on the cobbles, the naked man lunged, the curved blue steel held out straight before him. Its point went into the guard's belly an inch above the deepset navel and protruded out his back.

The guard screamed and dropped his blade. His hands clawed at the pain in his middle as he lunged forward, face down.

The pasha of Tripoli stared at his fallen gladiator. He was still watching the death throes when a soft hand touched his arm.

The woman had come forward from the goldsmith's stall at the first clang of the curving blades. Above the gold rim of her black silk veil, her yellow cat eyes glowed brightly, moving from the scimitars to the big, almost naked body of the American, then sliding sideways to the bronzed features of the pasha. Slyly, she had noted the faint touch of envy in his glance. Now she put a soft finger on his arm, so that he would turn and look at her.

Marlani Chamiprak was aware that she made a stirring figure, with the late afternoon sunlight on her thin, black silk trousers and long *yelek* of black satin threaded with gold that hugged her lissome body from throat to knees. Her veil was attached by silver pins to her glossy black hair. She was the favorite wife of Yussuf Caramanli, his *bash-kedin,* and her slightest whim was a command to him.

She said softly, "The infidel killed my personal body-guard, Yussuf."

"He shall be tortured with the bastinado on his naked feet, and the screws on his limbs, my love."

She pouted. "Oh, no! I would not want that." She added slyly, "He is a good fighter, is he not?"

The pasha sighed. "By the beard of the prophet! As good a man as I have seen since the days of my youth, when I fought beside Murad reis himself."

Marlani looked on the big Frank with overbright eyes. *Mashallah!* He was a handsome one, even in his starved state. There was pride in him, and a kind of inner wild-ness that sent little trickles of excitement down her slim brown legs. He was a different man from fat, bloated Kefas. It might be enjoyable, having him around the harem as her

12

personal bodyguard. Yussuf paid little enough attention to her any more, being too concerned with this war he had managed to get himself into with the United States.

She let her warm little hand come to rest on Yussuf's wrist. "Make him my guard, pasha effendi. Let the unbeliever take the place of Kefas!"

Yussuf Caramanli lifted his hard brown face to study the woman at his elbow. Marlani let her eyes smile up at this man who had deposed his brother Hamet for the pashaship of Tripoli less than a dozen years ago. She read the fierce pride in him, the ruthlessness and the cruelty. She knew also of the frustration that ate in him, because of the big American frigates like the *Constitution* that prowled the outer waters of the city and harbor he ruled. He was very angry now with the big blond American who had killed Kefas.

"You want me protected from all danger," she pouted, caressing his arm with slim fingertips. "And you said yourself this man can fight as well as Murad reis of blessed memory. Give him to me, Yussuf. Let him guard me, for you."

His nostrils flared. Yussuf Caramanli was confused, as he often was when this sly desert wife of his set her wits to obtain favors from him. Only in the most important matters did he ever seek to cross her, and then only sparingly. Now, as a gesture, he protested.

"But he is an infidel!"

"A hungry infidel," she reminded him, smiling beneath her veil. "If he will eat a rotten melon off the street, he would be grateful to whoever gives him better fare. He will be like a dog in his devotion."

The pasha glanced at the nearly naked American. He grumbled, "He should be made a eunuch."

"That would destroy his fighting abilities. You saw how easily he beat down poor, fat Kefas! If you really want to protect me, give me someone like that!"

The pasha grunted. What his *bash-kedin* said was true enough. To make a eunuch of this man would be to deprive him of a swordarm that might serve the Caramanlis with fanatical devotion. Still, he was an American, and Tripoli was at war with the Americans.

Marlani Chamiprak pressed closer. "Your enemies are not all Americans, remember! Your brother Hamet is not dead. He has many friends in Tripoli. Some night he may send

13

someone to kill me, knowing how dear I am to you. The nasrany would be a very tiger against such an attack."

The pasha of Tripoli studied the bone structure of the slave. He had a big, strong body, a body that could defend him as well as his *kedin*, if the need arose. It would not matter to the American whether he killed one Tripolitan or another. Yussuf rather thought that this yellow-haired slave might enjoy killing some of Hamet's friends, if they ever did attack him. Yussuf shivered with anticipatory fear, and looked closer at the big slave. That tall body would fill out with hard muscle when he ate something other than street refuse.

Yussuf Caramanli prided himself on his judgment. He said harshly, "Who owns you, nasrany?"

"Ali ben Sidi, the stone merchant."

"I will buy you from him. I will make you personal guard to Marlani. Do well, and you shall be rewarded well. Fail and—" The pasha shrugged. He said softly, "Have you ever seen what a lead-tipped knout can do to a man?"

The man in the dirty rag shivered. His bared back bore the scars of former whippings. The pasha smiled cruelly.

"What is your name, infidel dog?"

The arrogance of Yussuf Caramanli, before whose corsair fleets all the world appeared to tremble, brought a spate of fury into the starving man. He let the anger run along his veins, enjoying its feel after so many months of subservience. It was good to be half blind with clean rage again. Not the craze of almost madness that had been in him short moments ago—that was rash, and only brought destruction to a man. This anger was different; it was cool and it let a man think, and it was all the more deadly because of that.

Not since Ali ben Sidi had strung him up by his wrists and ordered his bare back lashed to a bloody froth, had he been this way. That had been three days after the U.S. *Philadelphia* had run aground on the shoals of the harbor of Tripoli.

The United States and the Barbary state of Tripoli had been at war in that mid-autumn of 1803, a war begun when Yussuf Pasha used an axe on the flagpole of the American consulate at Tripoli when that young nation across the Atlantic refused to join its European fellows in paying tribute to the corsairs.

A fleet under the command of Commodore Edward Preble had gathered at Gibraltar to blockade the North African coast. Under Captain Bainbridge, the *Philadelphia* ran the shoals and reefs of those treacherous waters, hunting corsair ships. On the last day of October, while chasing 'a small vessel standing in for the protection of the Tripolitan roadstead, the *Philadelphia* scraped across a reef.

Stephen Fletcher had been taken from the helpless frigate to the slave mart, and then to the stone quarries. When he showed stubbornness and fight, Ali ben Sidi had summoned his big slave master. Fletcher had been strung up by the wrists and lashed until his bare back was a bloody pulp.

The cuts of that whip had gone deeper than the flesh they marred. They taught him caution and prudence, and a seeming humility. He learned how to behave like a slave under the lash that night. Ali ben Sidi had no more trouble with him. He worked days in the stone quarries, and the nights he spent sleeping fitfully, dreaming of the Virginia plantation that had been his home, and of the fields of tobacco and cotton shifting in the breeze off the Shenandoahs.

The year and a half since the grounding of the *Philadelphia* added to the strength of his long thighs and lean middle, putting power in his chest and arms, ridging his back with swollen muscles. He was half starved all the time, and was never really free of the bite of hunger, and so in those hours when he was excused from the quarries, he took to scavenging in the streets.

Now, for the first time in many months, the starving man saw a chance to unleash his pride. He seemed to lift himself. His chin thrust forward.

"I am Stephen Fletcher," he said, "Lieutenant Stephen Fletcher, United States Marines."

The palace of the pasha of Tripoli lay southeast of the town, its high white walls brooding out across the blue waters of the roadstead. For uncounted years this palace had stood against the hot winds of the African *gibleh* and the lashing rains that came sweeping southward across the Mediterranean from Sicily. Dragut reis had anchored his galleys in these waters. In the twelfth century, Roger Guiscard had taken Tripoli from the Arabs with his Norman knights. In Roman times, the palace had been a fortress. The years between the days when Roman biremes swung to the swell of thé tides until now, when a sunset gun sounded

15

from the walls, had only whitened the building stone to a sepulchral pallor.

Fletcher found himself thinking of little but food as he walked betwen two surly brown guards into the palace. His stomach was a vast hollow between his loins and his ribcase. For food, he would guard the person of the seductive brown Marlani with any weapon Yussuf Caramanli chose. But deep down inside him, possibly at the hope this new life was opening to him, a tiny flame of rebellion stirred.

The harem quarters lay off the inner courtyard. Fletcher was taken to the harem guards' rooms, where he stripped the rag from his middle and bathed in warm water thick with suds. Soft towels were given him to dry his flesh. Clean for the first time in months, he donned loose muslin trousers and a linen *camyss*, with low slippers of yellow Moroccan leather on his feet. Around his lean middle went a girdle of copper discs, from which would be hung a curved scimitar on thin iron chains. Then he was taken before the keeper of the house.

Sinan ibn Ajaj was a big man, with a shaven head from which hung a black topknot wrapped with golden threads. His red vest, trimmed with gold brocade, enclosed a massive chest and paunch. Fletcher had the feeling that his bulk was deceiving. There was muscle under all that lard, his thick arms were proof enough of that. His fleshy face was creased now in a disapproving scowl, as he let his small black eyes run over Fletcher. He walked around him, his frown deepening.

The bald Turk grumbled at him. "You look well enough for a nasrany. Big, and thick in the shoulders. Plenty of room for solid muscle, once we put some meat and rice in your belly." His hand slapped hard at the muscles ridging the American's torso. He grinned, "That *cus-cus* will help you fight off any true believers who come slipping into the harem quarters at night. And don't believe they won't come, some time. Not to make love to the little *kalfas*, but to slip cold steel into Yussuf himself."

Fletcher looked interested. "Do they hate him so much in the city, then?"

Sinan ibn Ajaj grinned coldly. "Not most of them. But there are always a few hotheads willing to risk their necks to save another man's food from the fire. Remember, Yussuf drove out his brother Hamet, and became pasha in his

16

place. Hamet is no holy man, to ignore that affront. If he could, he'd cook Yussuf for a month over a bed of red coals. A month? Ten years! But Yussuf has the power and Hamet is a broken man."

He gloomed at Fletcher from under shaggy black eyebrows. "There are plots and counterplots cooking from the Grand Bazaar to the Land Port Gate, right now. Reason they haven't struck before is that Yussuf Caramanli keeps himself too well protected. Never lets down his guard, not once. But sometime he will and—*inshallah!* When that time comes, you'll have your bellyful of fighting, believe me!"

That was a prospect he would look forward to, Fletcher assured himself silently. Not alone for the sake of the action, which would serve to release some of the angers and frustrations that had been building up in him these past eighteen months, but because it would give him a chance to strike back at these Barbary seadogs. He was no scholar of history, but he knew the corsairs for a medieval anachronism, a throw-back to the time of the feudal robber barons. They roamed the Mediterranean as the White Company and others like them used to rove the land. They preyed on the helpless and the slow of keel. They robbed, taking what they would. And because it would cost their governments too much money to outfit a fleet against them, the European nations preferred to pay them tribute.

It may have been because their own liberty was so new that the young United States bridled at the conduct of these pirates. To them, the liberty of the sea was a dear and precious thing. Almost, Fletcher thought wryly, as precious as his own personal liberty.

Because his own liberty was so precious, he would die to save it. Now he was making the first step upward from the slave conditions of the stone quarries. As a bodyguard to the pasha's wife, he would gain a certain amount of bodily freedom. It was up to him to hoard and nourish that tiny seedling of liberty, until he could make it blossom, full grown.

To aid that growth, he must make friends here. To that end, he grinned in a friendly way and jabbed a thumb into the Turk's ribs. "For a brave man, you talk a lot, Sinan. My belly is as empty as the purse of a wandering beggar.

17

Is there no food at all in this hulk of stone you call a palace?"

Sinan moved to the arched doorway, beckoning Fletcher to follow. They went down a corridor tiled with marble chips in red and yellow. Fletcher had visited the Alhambra in Spain, during the cruise of the *Adams* in 1802. He found the interior of this palace, with its wall mosaics and gilt decorations, to be the equal of the delicate stone tracery and blue faience work of that citadel. His eye was caught by the glazed earthenware urns that lined the pillared gallery, and the silver-gilt plating of a great chest of blued wood that rested close beside a wall fountain.

It was then that he saw an inordinately thin man, with a red turban set awry on his head, scurry from the shadows across the tiled floor and into the shelter of a horseshoe arch. The man seemed a human scarecrow, with his striped barracan flapping loosely about his grotesque figure as he ran. One he turned his head and looked at the American, and Fletcher felt a cold shock pass over him at sight of those wild, reddened eyes.

Sinan growled. "Yon thing is called Yuvaz the Armless. The reason he looks so scrawny, like a fowl plucked bare for the pot, is that he's got no arms. Yussuf burned them off, just after he took the pashaship of Tripoli from his brother, Hamet Caramanli."

Fletcher made a retching sound in his throat and Sinan grinned, casting him a sly glance. "Empty belly gets sick easily, doesn't it? Yavuz was a good man, devoted to Hamet. Wouldn't take the vow to Allah to support Yussuf, though. Always claimed Hamet was the pasha. Yussuf had him thrown to the torturers. They cooked his arms and made him eat a little of the flesh. To save his life, Yussuf sent for an Arab physician from Cairo. He cut 'em both off, clear up to the shoulders."

Sinan spat. "Would have been a kindness to let him die. He's half mad. Can't even feed himself. But the pasha likes to have him around. Reminds him Hamet is still alive, planning vengeance or a return to power or whatever it is that deposed pasha's plan."

"Poor devil!"

"A poor fool! No man should be so loyal. What's it got him? Ah, here we are! Smell that food, man?"

The kitchen was an immense room fitted with a dozen

open hearths. Refectory tables groaned under silver platters loaded with oranges and plums, melons from Algiers and Tunisian figs. Two women in striped barracans were ladling out a thick stew filled with chunks of lamb and bits of yellow bread and vegetables.

Sinan swaggered forward, topknot swinging.

"Stir your fat legs, *sofradji!* My nasrany friend, the man who killed Kefas in fair fight this afternoon on the Street of Arcades, has an empty belly. The pasha has said he must be strong, to guard the *bash-kedin* and her women."

The women glanced at Fletcher from under heavily lashed eyes. They giggled, and while one came forward with a bowl of stew the other brought a long twist of barley bread.

"Don't throw your bodies at him, daughters of sin," Sinan growled. "He's almost as hungry for a woman as he is for that stew."

The two women were fat and greasy. One of them was old enough to be a grandmother. They squealed at the Turk's words, and scurried back to their hearths. Sinan straddled a stool and watched the American dip a spoon into the thick soup.

When he was done, Sinan called another woman to the table. "Didn't I tell you the nasrany was hungry, Rephia? Give him more!"

Fletcher ate five bowls of the stew and finished three lengths of the hard-crusted bread. He ate fig paste and a slice of sweetmeat before he admitted, as he swallowed the last few drops of the palm wine Sinan had poured for him, that he was hungry no longer.

Sinan looked at him with shining black eyes, nodding his head. "You ate well, for a Christian. By Allah! If you guard Marlani Chamiprak the way you wolf your food, Yussuf will make you a free man in a week. He values good service, does the pasha. Treat him well and his generosity will overwhelm you."

Fletcher put that thought away inside him as he got to his feet. "Come along, then. I'm anxious to discover how generous this Yussuf Caramanli can be."

With a grin on his lips and a roll to his walk, Sinan brought Fletcher up a flight of stone steps and out into the dying sunlight on the second courtyard. His thumb jerked upward at the grilled stonework of the harem windows.

"That's where you'll be quartered, up there behind that

19

latticework. You'll be surrounded with women. Pretty girls, not like those fat cooks down in the kitchen! Hotblooded Tauregs and pallid Spanish slaves. Turks. Greeks. Women of every nation you can name, and you not able to put a finger on any one of them."

Sinan paused and cocked a speculative eye at the big American. "Watch yourself, nasrany. They may be slaves and concubines, but they all belong to Yussuf Caramanli. If you're caught playing games with them, your death won't be a pleasant thing!"

"I'll be as indifferent to them as if I were a eunuch," Fletcher promised glibly.

Sinan chuckled. "They won't make it easy for you. Some of those little *kalfas* have been a long time without a man. They'll risk death by suffocation for a few hours of manly comfort. I tell you this because I've taken a liking to you. Guard your virtue better than you guard your life. It amounts to the same thing, in the harem."

As he walked at the heels of the Turk, Fletcher found himself thinking of his plantation home in Virginia, and of its pillared elegance. In the years of his rebellious youth, when he had been obliged to sit at a Monroe desk and add up columns of figures in the workhouse beside the stable portico, or journey to the ironworks near Baltimore in which his father owned a controlling interest, he had dreamed of something other than fields of tobacco and ledgers filled with monotonous numerals. Checking the slaves as they painted the washhouse or put fresh straw on the floor of the coachhouse, or riding Big Dan across hundreds of acres rolling fat with green tobacco, had been infinitely boring.

The ocean stretched wide and green from the mouth of Accokeek Creek, a day's ride from the manse. He would spend long afternoons staring at it, with Big Dan browsing contentedly on bunch grass twenty feet away. When the chance came to go aboard a training ship as a midshipman, he snatched at it. As a midshipman, he would see distant lands that were only names in books to him at the time. There would be no dusty ledgers, no tobacco fields or roaring blast furnaces to occupy his time. Later, he had been transferred to the marine corps, at his own request.

Fletcher smiled grimly. Instead of his dreams of adventure, he faced the reality of slavery. He wondered for a moment what his aristocratic father, gentleman planter that he was, might do in his place. Would he choose death to acting the slave for an unbaptised infidel? Or would he plan, as he himself planned, to play his part in such a manner that he would win over the confidence of his captors and perhaps, eventually, his freedom? Fletcher realized that a man made his own destiny, by his own acts. It was not his father who walked toward the harem quarters behind Sinan ibn Ajaj, but himself.

The food in his veins and the months of slave labor in the stone quarries of Ali ben Sidi began to work their spell. Strength came flooding into his body. He stretched a little, feeling confidence and sureness blossom in him.

The pasha of Tripoli sat on one of the hundred cushions thrown across a quarter of the tiled floor of his audience chamber. His legs in loose silk trousers were crossed under him. His brocaded kaftan jacket was covered by strings of seed pearls. His black beard had been freshly trimmed and scented.

He spoke swiftly with Sinan in a Turkish dialect that Fletcher could not follow. Whatever it was the bald Sinan told him, he grunted in approval. He lifted his hands and clapped.

A palace guard entered, carrying a lacquered swordcase in his hands. He knelt and set it before Yussuf Caramanli, who was regarding Fletcher all this while with a curious smile on his full lips. Reaching out with a slippered toe, he kicked the long teakwood case.

"Open it," he told Sinan. "Show the nasrany the sword that will be his only friend for the rest of his life."

It was a magnificent weapon, of blue Damascus steel, its curved blade inset with thin kufic scrollwork. The hilt was of silver on steel, and the haft was wrapped about with durable cording. Sinan brought it out into the lights of a hundred lamps and held it out to the Virginian.

"A good blade, Stefan. See for yourself."

Fletcher grasped the braided hilt, lifting the sword into his hand. It was light, but its steel was so finely made that he knew instinctively he had never before held such a weapon in his fist. Its blue, watered sheen was so bright that it seemed to glow in the lamplight.

Sinan saw that he was staring at the scrollwork, and leaned forward. "Its name is written there forever, infidel.

Dushman kush! The slayer of his enemies. Have you any enemies, Stefan?"

Fletcher brought his gaze up sharply, aware that there was mockery in the voice of the bald Turk. From Sinan, his eyes went to Yussuf Caramanli, who sat forward on his throne cushions, eying him with amusement.

"He does not know Mustafa reis, Sinan," chided the pasha with a smile.

"I know him," Fletcher growled. "He sold me to Ali ben Sidi."

The pasha laughed. "Ah, yes. You were one of the Americanos that went to my best sea captain as his share of the loot. Most of my other captains were glad to waive their rights for gold. Not Mustafa reis. He hates you Americans with a fine hate. Tell Stefan why, some time, Sinan."

Yussuf Caramanli stared thoughtfully at Stephen. "I did not know this afternoon that you were one of the men chosen by Mustafa reis. Otherwise I would have bastinadoed you and brought you back to the stone quarries for Ali ben Sidi to kill in any manner he desired, to teach his slaves the consequences of killing a royal guard. However, Allah saw fit to make me act without such knowledge. Now, of course, I am committed. It would never do to give you back, once I bought you. It would be a sign of weakness, and a pasha must never be weak. So you will take your post in the harem, to guard Marlani Chamiprak."

Losing interest, the pasha leaned forward to a silver platter filled with purple grapes. Idly, he drew a bunch into his hand and sat there cross-legged, nibbling at them, as Sinan took Fletcher down the length of the audience room.

As the big bronze doors clanged shut behind them, Sinan sighed and shook his head. "A lucky star watches over you, nasrany. Mustafa reis will not like what Yusuf has done. He will give anything to put you back in chains, or torture you to death in a public square. But Yussuf will not let him do that; it has become a matter of pride to him. But walk as if you walked on eggshells! One false slip, and even the pasha of Tripoli will not be able to protect you from him."

"I'll be careful," Fletcher promised, but Sinan only eyed him curiously and grunted.

"You aren't the careful kind!" the bald Turk growled, and clapped his heavy, meaty hands.

In the distance the patter of bare feet sounded along the tiled floors of the palace hall.

Sinan sighed, "I won't see much of you, once you go behind the seraglio doors. You'll live in a different world from me. There will be jealous women, and lusting women, and scheming women. Only a eunuch is able to live there without trouble settling around his ears. Make believe you are a eunuch, American!"

A slim Taureg girl, with hair like blackened copper hanging to her brown shoulders, came walking toward them. Silver hoops swung from her tiny ears. Her glowing eyes, their lids darkened with kohl, studied his big bulk. Beneath the thin *khalak*, that was a sheer mist of green silk, her body was naked. Her full breasts moved faintly to her breathing. Her legs were slim and brown, long and shapely, under the floating silk.

Sinan said, "Her name's Shellah. A Taureg girl, a slave. She sometimes acts as guide or messenger in the palace. She'll take you to the harem quarters."

The girl was smiling boldly, letting her dark eyes drift over Fletcher with calculating slyness. There was impudence in her smile and in her lazy stance. When Sinan shouted at her in Turki, she shouted back at him, baring tiny white teeth.

"Desert harlot!" grumbled Sinan. "Remember what I told you, Stefan. Don't let these little *kalfas* get their claws into you, or you'll wind up blind in chains, hung upside down over a rat pit! Remember! Now, go with Shellah."

It was not a difficult command to obey. The Taureg girl carried something of the wildness of the desert in the spicy smell of her thick hair and in the warm glow of the eyes. She glanced slyly at this big, yellow-haired man as she padded beside him, and she let the misty kalak slide a little, baring her supple brown back.

Her giggle came into the silence between them as they mounted the wide stairway to the harem rooms. Now the Taureg girl grew coquettish. Her arm brushed against him as they walked.

Once she said something in the Bedouin tongue that Fletcher did not understand. When she realized that he could not comprehend her desert jargon, she laughed softly. She spoke again, and though the words were strange, something in their inflection made Fletcher flush.

23

His hands closed on her wrist and he brought her to a halt, swinging her in against him. With one hand he caught the thick black hair, twisting his fingers in it, and held her face motionless.

"I don't know your game, little one," he told her, staring down into the bold eyes that never flickered, though his grip on her hair stung her scalp. "Maybe Sinan told you to act up, to test me. Or maybe it was the pasha, or even that favorite wife of his. I've been a slave a long time. Too long. I've almost forgotten that I'm a man, too."

He paused and grinned down at her soft red mouth. The palace was silent all about them. From where they stood, at the top of the tiled stair, Fletcher could see the length of the empty corridor before him. His pulse was beating faster now that her soft hips and legs were wedged so closely against him. Suddenly rebellion leaped in him—revolt against the subservience he must observe, against the irony of his position. Here he was, a strong man with a noble weapon at his side; but instead of fighting lustily for his country, he must waste his manhood protecting a group of pampered harem women.

"If you want to run to Sinan or the pasha or his wife," he went on conversationally, "and tell them what I'm going to do to you, go ahead. I have a sword at my hip again. This time they won't take me alive, to hang over any rat pit."

He kissed her roughly, hungrily, holding her head hard between hands, while his savagely seeking lips bruised her mouth. The Taureg girl took his kisses in a soft, sweet surrender. She melted against him with a supple twist of her slender body that told Fletcher she was enjoying this moment, whether or not she betrayed him later.

As he let her go, Shellah whispered something in her Taureg dialect, her eyes hot on his face. With fingertips tinted a bright red by henna paste, she drew her thin, revealing shawl about her body, and moved on. Her bosom was leaping with her hurried breathing, but the only sound was the musical tinkle of the silver chains about her slim ankles.

When they came to a door inscribed with geometric inlays and set with two-round gold hoops for handles, Shellah put her fingers on one of the grips and lifted her dark eyes. "Enter, Stefan. And do not worry, Shellah is no mewling spy, to go running when a man kisses her."

She saw his amazement at her knowledge of the English language, and paused, still holding the doorpull. "I was captured when I was very young, at the oasis of Kufra. They found me intelligent, and taught me many things. Your language was one of the things I learned. Now go in, and say no more of what happened between us."

The Taureg girl tugged and the door swung outward.

Fletcher stepped into a domed room, its walls ornate with delicate plaster friezes in bold reds and blues and golds. Tall archways led back into gloomy recesses, and the last red rays of the dying sun came thrusting through the iron fretwork of the windows. He saw low sofas, heaped heavily with pillows and silk cushions, an occasional table and coffer of inlaid teakwood, a few upholstered benches and ottomans.

Lying at full length on one of the low sofas, her right hand draped lazily from the cushions so that her fingers could scratch and fondle the head of a white kitten, was Marlani Chamiprak. Her gaze was fastened on the silken veils that floated from the ceiling overhead. As Fletcher stepped across the sill, she arched her slim body, revealing that her only article of clothing was a pair of loose, silken trousers of royal green.

Marlani said sweetly, "Did the nasrany give you any difficulty, Shellah?"

"No difficulty, highness," replied the girl, entering behind Fletcher and closing the door.

Apparently still entranced by the dangling lengths of red, blue and yellow silk floating in the eddies of air above her, the *kedin* laughed softly. "He is a disappointment. I was hoping that hot red blood ran in his veins. It seems I made a mistake."

Her hand came away from the kitten and gestured lazily. "Come stand before me, nasrany. I want to see what my new guard looks like."

Fletcher went to the foot of the divan and let her stare at him. Admiration shone in her yellow cat eyes as she examined his deep chest and bared midriff. He was a big man, Fletcher, towering tall and muscular among the scented cushions and silks. His height made Marlani look up at him, and now the American could read the wanton hunger in her eyes, the hidden desires and emotions that must be veiled everywhere but in the privacy of her harem boudoir.

25

The woman writhed, stretching. Laughter gurgled deep in her throat as she saw his eyes drawn instinctively to the hard brown breasts thrusting up at him. She whispered throatily, "You are mine now, Americano. You belong to me. Here in the selamlik my word is law. Even Yussuf does not interfere with what I do."

She came off the low, cushioned sofa with a flash of shapely brown legs and walked toward him, hips rolling easily, a smile twisting the corners of her red mouth. Lightly, she scratched her fingernails, sharply pointed and coated with silver dust, across his chest. Her yellow eyes brightened, glowing.

"He does not interfere at all! Whatever I do here, is my own business!"

Fletcher thought numbly that the pasha of Tripoli would make it *his* business if Fletcher dared to do what the bold yellow eyes invited him to do. For the first time since the *Philadelphia* went down, there was good food in his belly and clean clothes on his body. If this wanton with the kohl-darkened eyes and the musk-scented hair were to have her way with him—and the pasha learned of it—he would be strung up by his heels over a slow fire.

Marlani Chamiprak read something of this in his stony face. The yellow eyes narrowed. The red lips drew back a little, to show even white teeth. "You are a coward! You are afraid of Yussuf. And I thought all you Americanos were brave men!"

Marlani let the tide of her desire run wild in her, making no attempt to check it. Never before this moment had she felt like this. Never before had a big blond American stood in her boudoir, fighting for control, forcing his eyes away from the body she exhibited so shamelessly.

Before she had been wed to Yussuf Caramanli, Marlani had been a dancer at the court of Sultan Selim III of Turkey. Long ago she had learned the ways of pleasing men, and with her lessons had come an avid addiction to the art. She had been faithful to Yussuf, but since he had begun this stupid war with the United States, he had become more and more neglectful of her.

She laughed softly, throwing her head back. Then she swirled, arms spread wide, and went dancing about the room, her thin silken trousers billowing outward. She danced nearer to Fletcher, tripped across a cushion and fell against

26

him. Her upturned face was an inch below his chin, her honeyed breath fanning his lips as her cat eyes mocked him.

"Coward!" she whispered fiercely. "What are you afraid of? Put your arms around me! Make love to me, nasrany!"

He held himself as rigid as if he were at attention on the spar deck of the *Constellation,* his training ship. For one instant he stared down into her flushed, lovely face with its kohled eyes and long lashes, seeing the moist red lips waiting, parted. Then his gaze lifted until he was staring blankly above her brown hair at the Moorish windows of the haremlik.

He said heavily, "The pasha said I was to guard his wife against all harm. He said my life depended on it."

She whispered, "In the harem, my word is the law. Kiss me!"

She writhed against him, but he was as unmoving as a statue. Then Marlani Chamiprak drew back and snarled, like a savage cat. Her hand came up and her palm cracked hard against his cheek. Three times she hit him, until his cheek was an angry scarlet.

"You Americano fool! You shouldn't have made an enemy of me. It would have been better for you to have Yussuf angry with you, than me!" She paused for breath and slowly the rage gave way to a quiet slyness, brightening her eyes and curving her lips. "If you want it like this, with open war between us, very well. But remember, I fight as a woman fights!"

She turned on a heel and walked away. Just before she disappeared behind the archway curtains, she looked back over a bare shoulder. "I'll make you forget yourself yet, nasrany. When I do, I'll tell Yussuf you raped me! Pray to your gods that it will take a long time."

The curtain fell behind her, limply, and Stephen Fletcher was aware that sweat was standing out like jeweled beads on his forehead.

CHAPTER 2

It was the time of lamp lighting, one week after the day when he had killed Kefas on the Street of Arcades, that Fletcher was summoned before the keeper of the house. He found Sinan ibn Ajaj seated at a teakwood desk, its top inlaid with mother of pearl. There was a large leather bag in front of the bald Turk. At sight of Fletcher, Sinan dipped his brown paw into the coins that bulged the sides of the sack. He counted out a handful, and pushed them across the table top to the American.

"Your *alaik* coins, Stefan. There's a slave tavern run by Niccolo Gritti the Neapolitan, beyond the Street of the Sailmakers. You'll find your kind there, nasrany. Christian dogs. Maybe even some Americans. Have yourself some fun."

Fletcher stared, aware that puzzlement showed in his slack jaw and wide eyes. The Turk leaned back, thumbs hooked at his sash, grinning.

"Surprises you, doesn't it? All slave masters aren't as stupid as Ali ben Sidi! That's why we hand out *alaik*— slave money. Matter of fact, there's a little slave community right here in the heart of Tripoli itself. Gritti runs a tavern. Carapoulous the Greek owns an odd goods shop, where an Italian can buy himself some maccaroni, or a Frenchman some pastry. I understand they have little flags for homesick Americans, too. Buy yourself one. It'll make you feel better. And work better, too. The smart masters give their slaves a chance to let off steam by meeting at Gritti's Olive Tree, or the *Coq d'Or*. Do they lay plans to escape, there? What if they do?"

Sinan leaned forward, and his dark eyes blazed with mocking pride. "Where can they escape to, eh? The desert? They'd dry up and blow away inside two days! The sea? The corsairs own the sea hereabouts except where the cursed Americans sail their frigates! They'd bring 'em back and torture them in public. No, it doesn't do any harm to let the slaves meet. They can't go anywhere. They talk a lot and make plans that never come about, and are happier and healthier as a result. Their owners get more out of them. Everybody's better off, all the way around."

Sinan pushed the silver coins forward. "So take the money and enjoy yourself. You can get drunk on whisky—*mashallah!* what an infidel concoction!—if you want."

Fletcher walked out of the palace to the street. Dusk was settling along the shore of North Africa, bringing the glow of lamplight from deeply recessed windows in the white-walled shops and mosques. In the cool shadows he moved swiftly, passing a Berber tribesman newly out of the Fezzan desert sands, and a harem eunuch on his way to the sweet-meat shops.

There were a few corsair captains in turbanned helmets moving along the Street of the Sailmakers, readying equipment for fresh voyages upon the Mediterranean. Through the open doorways he saw the sellers of sails haggling over prices or displaying canvas to swarthy men with beak noses and spade beards, their left hands resting on the hilts of scimitars or curved daggers. American ships like the frigate *Constitution* and the schooner *Enterprise* maintained the blockade outside the harbor rocks, but the Mediterranean was a large sea, and the African shoreline boasted many little coves and inlets. Small feluccas and narrow barquentines could anchor unseen in the shelter of high rocks and tree-clad promontories. At night they could slip out into the sea and be a score of miles away by dawn.

The slave trade prospered at the hands of these ingenious sea captains. They brought their captives and their pirated loot overland from those hidden coves in camel caravans. Tripoli suffered from the patrolling of its coastal waters, by American ships, but not as much as it would have done without the hawk-faced corsairs.

They were anachronisms, these pirates—holdovers from the days of Barbarossa and Dragut reis. Time passes slowly along the coastal sands of Africa. Time forgot that in the outer world, robber barons were a thing of the past. Here under the lazy Tripolitan sun, men lived as they had lived during the days of the Holy Roman Empire. They did not know that men like Hargreaves and Arkwright were improving the art of spinning, and that James Watt and his steam engine were beginning to revolutionize a world. Their own world never changed. Their camel caravans were as they had been when Caligula was Emperor in Rome. Their stoves were a mere circle of stones, sometimes fastened together with a blob of mortar. The swords they used were the scimitars that had flashed against the Crusaders.

Yet these holdovers from a bygone day held the power of life and death over men who knew that civilization had left Tripoli behind in its little eddy of time. Chained in work gangs were men whose lips had tasted port wine in London's Red Cowl, who had purchased bohea tea in New York City's Hanover Square, or made bets at Ascot Downs on the horse races.

The big American grimaced, remembering Marlani Chamiprak. No man could tell that supple bit of temptation that her world was a lost colony in time! Her cat eyes would laugh at him, the way they laughed at Fletcher when she commanded him to stand guard on her person as her slave girls bathed her and anointed her with perfumes. To tempt him further, she had paraded her slave women before him, under the pretense of inspecting them for boils. Always she laughed at him, most especially when he turned away his face to stand facing the great double doors with their brass handles and kufic inscriptions.

Fletcher clenched his big hands into hard fists. Soon now, unless he could find some way out of this city, he would fall into the embrace that Marlani hungered for. And when he did that, and Yussuf Caramanli learned of it, as he would with the harem full of spies, he would be taken and tortured to death.

He shook his head against his gloomy thoughts, and lengthened his stride. Ahead of him now the wooden sign, bearing the likeness of an olive tree, creaked lazily on rusted chains. Beneath it was the doorway of Niccolo Gritti's grog shop, lighted by half a hundred brass oil lamps. Nearing the open door, he heard the sound of harsh laughter spilling out into the night.

He stepped inside and stood a moment beside the heavy wooden door hanging open on rusty iron hinges, letting his gray eyes move from the scar-topped counter that ran the length of the east wall, tiers of bottles and jugs behind it, to the refectory tables and benches that filled the big, wide room.

Men in rags sat cheek by jowl with men in satins and brocades. Men sat alone in gloomy corners to which the lamplight scarcely reached, or brooded sullenly over pewter mugs of rum and beakers of raw, hot whisky. An Italian whispered fierce oaths to a dark Spaniard beyond the first hanging brass lamp, while across the table from them, two Greeks with hoop earrings rolled dice with three Frenchmen. At the next table, four Englishmen murmured softly among themselves, homesick for the fogs of London.

Fletcher shouted, "Mark! Mark Avison!"

The men at the third table turned at sound of his voice. One of them, a tall man with a scar running from his left jaw to his shaggy blond brows, stood up.

"It's the lieutenant! Steve Flecher!"

They came in a rush, hands extended to thump him on back and chest, to take his hands and squeeze them, their faces wrinkled in delighted grins. He heard a nasal New England twang mix with the hard syllables of a New Yorker, and the soft drawl of Jabez Plummer, who was from Georgia. They tugged him to the table and shoved him down.

"Fretta! Fretta!" shouted Mark Avison, whose father had been killed at Yorktown, "Gritti, damn your eyes! Fetch us rum. Jamaica rum"

Avison swung a leg over the bench, straddling it, slapping Fletcher on the back. He was a big man, thick-chested and tall, with long and powerful arms. In the little New England village where he had been born and raised, he had been a blacksmith. He pretended to be ashamed of the thick yellow curls on his head. In a hoarse, deep voice he asked, "What's with you, Steve? Last time I heard you were breaking your back over quarry stone!"

He told them of his luck. At mention of his street duel with fat Kefas, they banged the table with their fists.

"No man as good with cold steel as you, Steve, in all the corps!"

"Nor the navy, either!"

"Ha! I'd give a year of my life to have seen it!"

When Nicholas Gritti came with his battered copper tray and the beakers of oily rum atop it, he was introduced to Fletcher, and made to stand treat for the return of this man from the grave. Gritti put the pewter mugs down with a grin, but shook his head at the invitation to drink.

"Some of us must keep a clear head, in case of trouble. Drink my share, all of you."

They cheered him and huddled among themselves. Now Fletcher learned for the first time how the *Philadelphia* came to be burned where it swung at anchor in the roadstead. Less than four months after its capture, Lieutenant Stephen Decatur, with a command of sixty sailors and eight marines, had brought the sloop *Intrepid* under cover of darkness into the harbor.

"Sneaked up like a water snake!" said Avison.

"Boarded her and put her heathen crew to the sword, every last manjack of them!"

The New Yorker, Caleb Framingham, chuckled grimly, a rare smile lighting his thin, tense countenance. He was a tall man, lean and wiry. There was a Satanic turn to his dark, dramatic features. He had a habit of hunching forward and craning out his neck so that the man to whom he listened felt Framingham was mocking him. He said now fiercely, "Then they put the torch to her! Near broke my heart to see her rigging go up with red tongues eating it away, and more flames at her catheads and the waist!"

A small man twisted forward on the wooden bench. His eyes half lifted, then fell shyly to the bare-topped table, moving his rum mug in small circles. This was Ned Brunner, ship's carpenter. His eyes were a cold gray, and his smile was thin and derisive. His comments were often waspish, but his fellows liked him, for they realized it was mostly shyness that made him sharp and critical.

"I was glad and sorry, both at the same time," he said slowly. "Glad Decatur was burning her so the heathen couldn't use her against her own kind, and sorry she had to go like that."

"A good ship, she was," nodded Avison.

"A proud one, too," smiled Framingham, who had been first mate. "She'd have been glad to die like that, knowing she'd not have to use her guns on Americans!"

"The *Philadelphia!*" said Brunner, lifting his cup high.

They echoed him, and drank. Then they hunched closer, telling Fletcher of their experiences since the *Philadelphia* had run aground. Now for the first time, he learned that Captain William Bainbridge and his crew had been imprisoned in the castle and that they had been robbed of watches and coats and other valuables. Some had been given a house in which to live while others remained at the palace itself, to be held there for ransom. The English and Danish consuls had been most helpful, bringing needed food and clothing to them.

William Bainbridge was a heartbroken man, they told him. The letters he wrote home to his wife Susan had been filled with melancholia and anxiety. The money dispatched to him to care for the crew had cheered him a little, but his despondency was soul deep.

"Pasha's asking five hundred dollars a head for us," grinned Framingham. "Never knew I was worth so much!"

Mark Avison chuckled. "He's changing his tune a little. One time, he wanted three million dollars for peace. Now he's reduced that to a hundred and fifty thousand."

The men were philosophical about their capture and imprisonment. "Way I look at it is," said Brunner seriously, "I'll be here a few years. Make the most of it. Why not? They don't treat us too bad. Let us walk around, even give us the money our folks send from stateside."

None of them had any thought of escape, but then, none of them had a yellow-eyed woman waiting for him to make the one move that would put him irrevocably into her power.

"We could all get away, you know," Stephen said suddenly. "It wouldn't be too hard."

Their eyes watched him. No one moved. It seemed as if they stopped breathing. Fletcher drained the last of his rum and shoved the empty beaker out into the middle of the table. "There's no place to escape to. That's why we can do it."

"You talk in riddles, Steve!"

"Our pagan masters are so confident we're helpless that they let us meet in slave taverns like this one. They know we must talk of escape. What man wouldn't? Yet they do nothing to stop us. There are no guards, no spies."

"There's the desert and the sea," said Avison. "I've taken thought on it, Steve. Between the two, give me clear water and a keel under me."

"Aye," growled Brunner, "that's for me, too. No dying of heat with only sand to swallow for my thirst."

Fletcher hoped to be given more and more time to himself as he proved himself worthy to the pasha. His position in the castle gave him opportunities none of the others would have. He might even find a boat, a little tender with a hole in a thwart for a small mast, and a sail, he explained.

"How?" asked Framingham, his eyes gleaming.

He told them of the armless Yuvaz. "I'm not so sure he's as insane as they think. He hates the pasha. He might do something to spite him."

Framingham scowled into his empty cup. "Something like finding you a ship, eh? And a cask or two of fresh water, and some food! It listens good, Steve. Real good. So good I'm almost ready to let myself hope."

The Boston man stood up and howled at Gritti. "More rum, Nicco, lad. On the double! Now, with no excuses!" He sat down and stretched his legs. "It may take money," he mused.

Fletcher took out his leather purse and showed them the

33

gleaming silver coins. "A little pay to make a slave happy. Makes him feel more like a man, I guess. There'll be more of this coming my way. I've no expenses. I mean to keep my throat dry so's I can wet it in a free port."

He put the coins back into the sack and drew the strings taut. Then he thrust the pouch under his belt and stood up. "Take thought on it, lads. It's a chance the good Lord's given us. I mean to take advantage of it, when the tide's ripe. If you're willing to risk the public torture against dropping anchor in a free port like Malta or Messina— join me!"

Marlani Chamiprak walked back and forth before the American slave who was now her personal bodyguard. She wore thin black silk trousers embroidered in silver and bound at waist and ankles with tiny gold chains. From her midriff to her throat, a thin gauze veiled her flesh, while a short jacket covered her bosom and upper arms. Slippers of crimson velvet were on her feet. She made a barbaric picture as she moved back and forth and around the rigid Fletcher, her unloosened veil fluttering from her head.

"You've been in Tarabulus al-Charb for one month, nasrany. Tell me, do you like your service?"

Fletcher said, "Why shouldn't I like the hand that feeds me, and that gives me soft cushions to sleep on? The pasha is my little father."

Already he spoke in the flowery manner of the court Turk. Hearing the guttural sounds of high Turki, his tongue unconsciously mimicked its inflections.

"Tcha!" exclaimed Marlani softly, coming to a halt before him. "Whose ears are those lies for? You must hate it here, doing my bidding. And I'm glad you hate it. Glad!"

Her laughter bubbled up, strong and confident. "How long will it take me to turn you from a statue into a man? Until you need the comforting I can give you? Until that need is so great you'll forget Yussuf and his powers of life and death?" She came a little closer and her hand gripped his forearm. As he let his eyes meet her gaze, he saw the yellow eyes almost feverish in their hunger.

She pressed against him. "Perhaps we need other women to tempt you. You've seen nothing in the harem lovely enough to make you forget the tortures Yussuf will invent, when he learns you've made love to his favorite wife! Then

34

we shall go to the slave market. I myself will pick out the new girls!"

Fletcher groaned inwardly. How many days had he stood at the harem door, while Marlani Chamiprak, laughing softly from the cushioned sofa where she lay stretched in indolent nakedness, paraded her female slaves before him. He had lost count of the nights when he had been forced to stand above the pool where the *kedin* bathed, her gaze always intent on his bronzed face. Her treatment of him was a kind of torture in itself. She could not guess how near he was to cracking now, how near to forgetting everything but this woman and her desires, how near to gratifying them.

He made himself say coldly, "It will be a waste of time."

The breath hissed between her lips as fury swelled the veins under her smooth, coppery skin. "Will it be a waste of time, Stefan? It will be an interesting experiment to see what a waste it will be!" Then she was whirling, striding away from him, clapping her soft palms together.

"Ibrahim! Saud! Attend me. The curtained palanquin!"

The sea wind was blowing from Italy across the dark blue waters of the Mediterranean as Fletcher brought the little cortege out into the Street of Arcades. Under the cool shadows of the arches, sellers of Mosul muslins and Egyptian cotton goods, Baghdad damasks and ivory from distant China vied here with men showing crystal ware from Syria and fine silver plate from Cairo. Fletcher knew that only half these treasures had been brought overland, by camel caravan from Egypt and Morocco. Most of it had come from the holds of slow merchantmen and freighters worried into surrender by the corsairs of Tripoli.

The Street of Arcades was a wide avenue. Down its length, one could see the high white walls of the castle, and the glittering white column tipped in green with a gold crescent that was the minaret of the Caramanli mosque. The little group walked slowly, with Fletcher striding at point, the round shield at his back catching the sunlight, his Damascus scimitar jangling faintly in its scabbard chains at his every step. The palanquin carried by four gigantic Somalilanders was painted green and red and coated thick with gilt, its gold brocade curtains pulled back to let the salt breeze wash across the reclining figure of Marlani Chamiprak.

Ahead of them was the great square that was the slave bazaar. From its white walls, thick velvet canopies protruded, hung on long iron poles, extending out into the street. On raised stone platforms, some of which were perfectly round to allow more buyers of humanflesh to crowd about, the slaves were displayed, weighted down by iron ankle chains. Screened pens stood to one side, where other slaves waited their turn on the stone blocks.

A *dellal* was shouting his wares in a singsong voice as the captives came into the square. Men turned idly to look at them. On seeing the Caramanli palanquin, they drew back, to afford the *kedin* of the pasha a good view of this sale of a naked Bantu giant.

"See the muscles on his arms," droned the slave seller. "He is worth his weight in diamonds to a good master. Think of the stones he can lug for building. Think of the protection he will be when trained to use a scimitar!"

A lesser auctioneer came running to the litter. This was Fletcher's clue to move forward, to interpose his bulk between the body of Marlani Chamiprak and any possible shamshir blade or dagger point.

Head bobbing, his dark face wreathed in a smile, the *dellal* cried, "It is the grace of Allah that brings you this day, most ardent of Kedins! Only last evening, Kaisar reis himself brought in two ships, laden heavy with captives."

Marlani Chamiprak said lazily, "Allah have you under his eyes, *dellal*. I come seeking girl slaves. Strong ones. Women with beauty in their faces and in their bodies."

The auctioneer kissed his fingertips and bent low, so that his red turban was in danger of falling off. "Women of paradise I have, rose of beauty! Dark girls of Malta, and olive lovelies from Greece and Italy. There is also—" the *dellal* slanted his eyes sideways at the big Fletcher—"a very pretty girl from America."

Marlani did not miss the start that made Fletcher's scabbard chains jangle faintly. She sat up among her litter cushions and, with the bare left arm of Fletcher to help her, came to her slippered feet.

Her thin yashmak fluttered to her breathing. "Bring out the women, *dellal*. Reserve the American until the last. I mean to have her."

When the auctioneer was gone into the screened compound, she leaned closer to Fletcher, rich perfumes of Araby emanating from her braided black hair and from the gold brocade of her tight vest. "How would you like to see an American girl again, nasrany?"

Her laughter, as she moved ahead of him with taunting hips, was mocking.

It was then, as Fletcher was striding at her elbow, that he saw the face. It came up in front of him as it had come in dreams: the high, bridged nose, the skin like smooth brown mahogany, the bald head with the tuft of long black hair that lent a barbaric splendor to the man. Mustafa reis! The man who had come aboard the *Philadelphia* and singled him out for the stone quarries!

A flowing barracan of striped Decca muslin swathed his tall, wiry body as he pushed so easily through the throng about the trading blocks. There was an insolent pride in his dark eyes and in the casual recklessness with which he pushed men from his path. Between his curled mustache and spade beard, his lips were thin and hard. He looked with hate at the American, as he bowed to Marlani Chamiprak.

"I gaze with pleasure on the *kedin* of my pasha," he said softly. "Perhaps his favorite wife is wiser than Yussuf. Let me buy this American filth who has won the eye of our esteemed pasha, and—"

Marlani Chamiprak lifted her hand. "It was our eyes and not those of Yussuf he caught, Mustafa reis. Since then, he has behaved as befits a slave. Be assured, I will not sell him."

The captain bowed low, but the rigidity of his back told Fletcher he was not done. He moved away a little, and stood brooding.

The *dellal* brought out women from Crete and Greece, dark girls from Syria and blonde Milanese from the north of Italy. There was a pretty Frenchwoman, and three Spanish senoras. Marlani Chamiprak bought them all.

The *dellal* said, bowing low, "We have for this last but best offering, an American woman. A girl taken off the *Boston Lady* less than a week ago by the great Mustafa reis." He turned and waved a hand.

The pen screen lifted. A naked woman came out into the African sunlight, walking proudly with her head held high, long black hair forming a shawl that spilled down over slender shoulders and across her supple back. From under

37

long black lashes her dark eyes lifted calmly to the sky. It was as if she walked in the privacy of her own boudoir.

Black hair and white skin, the grace of long legs moving easily to the faint sway of rounded hips, made the staring Moslems cry out in admiration. When the girl came to a stop on the worn tiles of the slave block dais, the *dellal* swung her around to face the *kedin*.

Fletcher started as he felt those blue eyes staring down at him. Their lashes flickered faintly, and for the first time, shame painted a slow flush upward from her round breasts into her throat and cheeks.

Eve Doremus felt a tiny chill of despair stabbing through the red shame that flooded her cheeks. For the first time since she had been dragged screaming and fighting off the foredeck of the *Boston Lady*, she realized what was happening to her. It was like waking suddenly from a particularly terrifying dream and discovering it to be true. Her entire life had been so prim, so sheltered and protected! There had always been the Doremus name on which to rely in Boston, and her maiden aunts to soothe her fears and worry.

Now she stood alone and unclad before a hundred men, in the great slave mart of Tripoli. She thought, I should die, right here and now, of shame! But she was not dead; in fact, she felt excitingly alive and healthy. As an awed hush fell across the buyers in the big· square, the girl realized that it was in tribute to her beauty. Even as she wished for the ground to open and swallow her, something feminine inside her knew a touch of pride.

She shrugged faintly and tilted her chin high as the *dellal* cried exultantly, "How much am I bid for this houri out of Paradise? See the texture of her skin, the richness of her black hair! Walk, nasrany girl, and let them see the grace of your body. A—"

Marlani Chamiprak gestured. "A hundred silver dinars, father of windbags."

A sigh went across the square. A voice called, "Two hundred aspers!"

"Five hundred gold aspers!"

There was savagery and exultation in this last voice. Its tone drew all eyes, except those of Marlani Chamiprak and

38

Stephen Fletcher, to Mustafa reis. The corsair was grinning wolfishly, letting his gaze assess the ivory flesh of this nasrany girl. Mustafa reis thought, If the man is out of my reach, the woman is not! He was allowing his imagination to riot over the coming night, when the pale girl with the black hair would be brought to the low, wide divan of his bedroom. She would be wearing golden anklets and dangling earrings, a rope of pearls and a gauze skirt. A tongue came out to lick his lips as Mustafa reis started forward to claim his purchase.

"A thousand gold aspers!"

Mustafa reis whirled around. That was the voice of Marlani Chamiprak bidding against him! What in the name of Allah the Compassionate was she doing, bidding such a fortune on a girl slave? He came striding toward her, hand uplifted to halt the ecstatic *dellal* in his singsong incantations.

"By the beard of the Prophet!" the corsair hissed. "Has Shaitan stolen your wits, Marlani? What do you want with such a one?"

The *kedin* smiled faintly. "I have no American women in my harem. I want one as an—experiment."

Mustafa fell back a step, his mouth gaping open with shock. "For an experiment you would spend a thousand gold aspers?" he choked out, his face darkening with anger. "It pleases the *kedin* to mock me!"

Marlani Chamiprak smiled more fully. Her slant eyes went from her Franka to the corsair captain. "Mockery is the furthest thing from my thoughts, Mustafa! But I will not let you buy the American girl, just as I will not sell you the American man."

Mustafa hesitated, not knowing whether to beard the rage of his pasha by bidding up the price of the white woman, or to bow to the inner voice that counseled him that discretion was the finest part of valor. His wide shoulders shrugged elaborately, making the elegant gold braidwork of his white wool cloak rustle faintly.

"I bow to the wisdom of my pasha and to the beauty of his *kedin*," he murmured. Then he swung on Fletcher. "As for the Christian pig—"

He spat full into Fletcher's face.

For a moment, the American stood stunned. Then he swung savagely, his big fist traveling only a scant eight inches. The blow caught Mustafa reis under his bearded jaw and drove him backward, heels scraping the cobbles of the square, to fall heavily. A fold of his kaften hung limp in the air a moment, then settled lazily across his knees. Mustafa reis did not stir.

"You utter fool!" hissed Marlani Chamiprak.

Fletcher shook himself, his blinding anger fading before a sharp dismay. The high pride of him, born and fostered in Virginia plantation life and welded into a way of life during his years on the *Constellation* and the *Philadelphia* during his military service, was a parasite inside him, governing his actions. Too late, he realized what that pride had done. Yussuf Caramanli would give him now to this corsair captain, and probably add in the gift of the American girl as well, to soothe Mustafa's injured vanity.

The Tripolitan merchants were assisting Mustafa reis to his feet. His eyes were glassy and his knees shook under him.

"Wallahi!" whispered a gem seller who was here to buy himself a *kalfa* whose warm thighs and full bosom might make him forget his recently deceased wife.

"He struck with the speed of the hunting cheetah. Saw you ever such a blow?"

A man laughed. "I did not see it. Neither did Mustafa reis!"

"I am sorry for the nasrany. Mustafa will take the rest of his life to kill him! Only this morning he was telling me of a new torture. . . ."

Marlani Chamiprak whispered furiously, "You hear? You hear?"

Fletcher heard. And he reflected again on the fate that had made him first a slave, a carrier of heavy stones, then reduced him to stealing refuse off the streets for food. That same fate had chosen to put a sword on his hip, but denied him the chance to use it honorably. Now if a lingering death by ripping hooks and slow fire lay at the end of his road, it was only one last twist of fate's cruel hand.

The *dellal* came down off the round block, bowing to the *kedin*.

40

"Gracious lady of our noble pasha, shall I close the bidding?"

They were leading Mustafa reis away from the square. Marlani Chamiprak watched him go a moment, then nodded. "Wrap her in some garments and bring her, with the other women, to the palace gates before sundown. The gold will be ready for you then."

With a warm hand on Fletcher's arm, the *kedin* moved to her palanquin. As she slipped onto the cushions, she hissed up at the American, "You fool! You've spoiled everything now. It was all right to play the soldier with me, and be proud as Shaitan, for I enjoyed the game—the bigger the pride, the more pleasure for me in bringing you to my harem sofa!"

She paused and her little brown hand trembled as she put it on his forearm. Her yellow eyes blazed hotly, and her supple body shook. "But now you'll bed with hot irons and sharp hooks for the next few weeks. You fool!"

Sinan ibn Ajaj was only slightly less disturbed when he learned what Fletcher had done to Mustafa reis. "You're a madman!" he declared, stalking back and forth in the selamlik antechamber. "All nasrany are madmen. With the life of a harem guard before you, with only the trouble of walking where the *kedin* walks to bother you the rest of your days, you hit a corsair captain! Insh'allah! Tired of life you must be, indeed!"

The keeper of the house grunted and shrugged. Muttering in Turki under his breath, he took Fletcher up a flight of tiled stairs to a small wooden door set with a brass latch. Sinan twisted the door handle and pushed the door open.

A room with bare white stone walls and a ceiling seamed with cedar was flooded with red fire from the dying sun. A low bed, formed by short sandalwood legs and ropings of Syrian hemp, stood against the wall. It was covered with fat cushions, and a spread of worn and frayed silver brocade. A low table, inset with bits of mother of pearl, held an ewer of palm wine and a platter of figs.

"Your prison," growled Sinan, "until Yussuf gives you to Mustafa!"

As he stared out over the bubble domes of the Tripolitan mosques from the recessed window of his little cubicle,

41

Fletcher felt despair growing in him. He remembered his comrades at the Olive Tree, off the Street of the Sailmakers, and the hopes he had aroused. He had spoiled all that with his hot Virginian temper.

CHAPTER 3

Yuvaz the Armless scurried like a frightened rat beside the white expanse of the garden courtyard wall. His sharp teeth were clamped down hard on a great iron key. Under his plain woolen robe his heart hammered with wild exultation. At last the plans over which he had nursed his pain and his burned arms were bearing fruit.

Beyond that street gate, the key to which he held in his teeth, men were waiting for his words in an eagerness that matched his own. Men had worked with loving care sharpening slim daggers to let the life all the more easily from the body of Yussuf Caramanli. Haste was mixed with that care, for all Tripoli knew that its pasha was readying his ship, the *Burak*, for a sea voyage. Once the *Burak* raised its anchor, no man could tell when Yussuf Caramanli would return, or whether those cursed Americanos in the big frigates would kill him on the sea. The pleasure of his pasha's death was something that the armless one had promised himself for a long time. It would not be prudent to wait much longer.

Yuvaz came to a stop, his turbanned head tilted slightly, to listen to the night sounds floating on the sea wind off the roadstead. He heard the faint giggle of harem girls, and the measured tread of a guard on the parapet high above. Somewhere, fingers were plucking out a muted tune. Ordinary sounds, little sounds the palace made on a uneventful night. For a long moment, Yuvaz went on listening.

Reassured, he ran hurriedly along the mud wall to the door that led onto the street. He bent his head, still gripping the key.

Yuvaz knelt down. Working his head sideways, he slid the key into the lock. He felt the pin miss and slip. Frantically he tightened the grip of his teeth and raised his head slightly. Now the bits slid in and took hold.

When the key was securely in the lock, he paused, leaning back on his calves to rest. He gulped in mouthfuls of the cool air, knowing his brow was beaded with nervous sweat. Then he bent his head again, and gripped the large quartrefoil of the key in his teeth. Carefully he twisted his head, and the lock opened. His cheek against the latch lifted it, and door swung open. Yuvaz got to his feet and stood there, smiling grimly.

"None will suspect Yuvaz the Armless of this treachery! How can a man without arms or hands open a locked door? No, Yuvaz. You are safe."

He went out into the night, his slippered toe dragging the door shut behind him.

Sinan ibn Ajaj came for Fletcher after the evening meal-time. He pushed his bald head with its dangling topknot through the open door of the little room and flashed white teeth in a wicked grin.

Fletcher lay stretched on the bed, hands behind his neck. On a small ebony table was the platter that had held his meat square and eggs. The big goblet that had been filled with palm wine was empty.

Sinan came into the room, one shaggy eyebrow uplifted.

"You're not one to worry overmuch about the death by red hot pinchers and sharp razor hooks, Americano! Eh, well! Nobody ever said you were a coward."

"Has the Pasha sold me to Mustafa reis?"

"More than likely. They're in the audience hall now. Yussuf sent me to bring you there."

Fletcher swung his legs over the edge of his low bed. It had been a good month, this last, except for the fact that he was a slave. Good food three times a day, and no duty to shackle him down except the task of stalking around after Marlani Chamiprak with a scimitar on his hip.

"All good things come to an end," he told the Turk.

Sinan watched him with bright eyes. All along he thought this nasrany giant was a madman. Now he knew it. He went to death by torture—slow torture that would take more than a month to kill him, if he knew Mustafa reis—with a grin curving his lips. Grudgingly, Sinan felt admiration dawn in him.

43

Almost respectfully he said, "Come with me, Christian."
As they walked side by side down the long gallery and the
wide stair beside the harem quarters, Sinan grumbled, "I'm
sorry, Stefan. I'll miss you. For all that you're an infidel,
by Allah, you're a man!"

Sinan paused at the arched horseshoe door of the audience
hall. His big hand at Fletcher's shoulder shoved the American into the long room.

Carpets lay thick on the tiled floor. At the far end of the
room, on a dais built of marble and covered with Aubusson
carpets and Persian rugs, Yussuf Caramanli sat on his
cushioned throne, crosslegged. A baldachin of ivory and
marble towered overhead, dwarfing the pasha and the corsair
captain who stood rigid and proud before him.

Fletcher found his footfalls making loud sounds in the
stillness. Under his ribs, his heart thudded so hard he
thought it must be reverberating through the long hall,
too. He came to a stop, to find Yussuf Caramanli smiling
grimly at him.

"Mustafa reis tells me you hit him with your fist this
afternoon, nasrany. That was a very foolish thing to do.
Especially since Mustafa offers to buy your bondage for
double the price I paid Ali ben Sidi."

Ever since he had been put behind the locked door of his
room, Fletcher had been thinking hard. Now he bowed, and
smiled a little. "As always, you speak truth, father of
wisdom. I did what you say. I hit the captain. But I only
acted in defense of the Caramanli name."

Mustafa reis cursed hotly and swung around on a heel, his
dark eyes glowing. Even his perfumed brown beard seemed
to writhe in his fury. "The Christian filth lies in his teeth!
I said no thing to insult my pasha!"

Fletcher faced the infuriated corsair, willing himself to be
calm. "The captain reis did worse than that. He showed
his scorn of his lord by spitting on his property."

A silence fell in the audience hall.

Yussuf Caramanli leaned back, and sighed deeply. He
turned his arrogant eyes toward the corsair captain. The
pasha realized that he had never liked this stiffnecked
Mustafa reis, whose raids on Christian shipping were always so successful and so profitable. Of the fact that jealousy

might enter into his feeling, he took no heed. Concerned only with his pride and his name, Yussuf saw in his arrogance that Mustafa reis might conceivably become a threat to him. More than one corsair captain had elevated himself to the pashaship on the ladder of his sea victories. He himself had won it from his brother Hamet by revolt.

What Yussuf had done to Hamet, Mustafa could do to Yussuf. To allow Mustafa reis this opportunity to flaunt himself in the eyes of his brother captains was not to be thought of. Slowly he said, "The nasrany is a very judge, a kadi of the law. I am ashamed to admit that he teaches me my royalty. A royalty that my captains delight in ignoring. Or worse!"

Mustafa reis breathed heavily. His brown hands opened and closed at his thighs like the talons of a hunting eagle. He burst out harshly, "There has been no thought of disloyalty!"

"You spat upon my property. It is the same as spitting on me!" The pasha allowed the words he spoke to bolster his anger. The more he thought about this thing that had been done, the angrier he became. He leaned forward from the waist and hissed his words.

"Must a slave teach me that my goods are sacred, as I am sacred? Thank Allah that my slave defends my name on the streets of the city I rule! In defending his person, that belongs to me, he defended me! Mustafa reis, you spat on me!"

The corsair captain poised a moment between open defiance and abject submission. Only too well did he know the power of this man who sat high on his throne cushions throwing words at him. The temptation to defy Yussuf Caramanli in his towering rage was little short of suicidal. He had none of his men at his back, while the palace swarmed with the pasha's guards.

And so, in his humility, Mustafa reis hung his handsome head, so that the silver oil cressets threw their reflections from his shaven skull. "Accept my apology, Yussuf Caramanli! It was without thought that I did this deed. I intended no insult to you and to what belongs to you. On the beard of the Prophet, I swear it!"

The pasha glowered. Mustafa reis was too good a sea

captain to punish overhard. In the interests of his people, he must know magnanimity. He said sullenly, "How can I be sure this will not happen again, and again, until my name is no more than a laughing stock in the market places?"

Mustafa reis stood with his head lowered. He said harshly, "I have three chests filled with gold coins that I took from a Portuguese ketch. My slaves will bring the chests to the palace, as proof of my innocence, and of my allegiance."

The pasha allowed himself to be as generous as his captain. His hand waved, the big emerald on his forefinger glinting with green fire. "I am pleased with Mustafa reis. I accept this evidence of good faith. Forget this vengeance on the infidel. He is only the dirt beneath your slippers. Only the slave who guards the person of my *kedin*."

Mustafa reis whispered that he would follow the advice of his pasha, but the veins were swollen in his temples and his eyes glowed with the fury in him. Watching Mustafa, Fletcher knew that his body had been spared unutterable tortures only by the pride of Yussuf Caramanli. As long as Yussuf lived, Fletcher was safe.

When the corsair captain was gone, after a long, hard look at Fletcher, the Pasha frowned down at him from his height of cushions. There was puzzlement and curiosity in the stare he directed at the American. It was as if Yussuf Caramanli asked himself how it had come about that this man stood before him now, alive and well.

Curiously he murmured, "Before you entered the audience hall, I had as good as sold you to Mustafa reis. I ask myself, is this my destiny, my kismet, that keeps you safe by my side? You are a sly man. You have sharp wits as well as a strong back. How will you use those wits and that strength? To aid or to harm me?"

Fletcher stood motionless, not quite believing in the luck that had left him stand here with the pasha of Tripoli. By rights, Mustafa reis should be dragging him off now to his own house, into the dungeons where every known form of torture instrument was rumored to be kept always shining. Instead, he was discovering that Yussuf Caramanli was grateful to him.

The pasha said, "I must believe that Allah has sent you to help me. I believe in my fate, my own destiny. Did Allah not

46

side with me against Hamet, when I brought him down from the throne? And believing in my fate, I must also make sure you believe in me and my cause."

Yussuf Caramanli clapped his hands. Sinan appeared in the doorway. His eyes bulged in his head when he saw Fletcher standing alone before his pasha. He sidled forward, forgetting to bow in his amazement. The loud laughter of Yussuf roused him to his senses.

Summoning Sinan to his feet, Yussuf told him what had happened. "Is he not a very kadi, Sinan? Eh? Heard you ever such an argument? Restore Stefan his scimitar. Then fetch in the slave girls. I'm going to make a present of one of them to the Americano. He's been virtuous too long in that harem upstairs!"

Yussuf roared his laughter to the vaulted ceiling. His face was flushed with pleasure. Almost childish in his sudden enthusiasms, he could be swayed from hate to affection by a word or a look. Now he was excited as a bridegroom on his wedding night.

He called out to Sinan, "Bring all the slaves, even the ones the *kedin* bought today in the slave market."

Fletcher tensed, thinking of the American girl. Yussuf saw the betraying quiver of his muscles and roared. "Ha? One of those new ones took your eye? Eh? Eh? Tell me."

"An American girl. The girl Mustafa reis wanted to buy."

"Good, good!"

If he could get this man to mate with one of his own kind, he might forge a chain of loyalty in him yet! Yussuf Caramanli knew men, and the emotions that men felt for other men. Now that he was convinced the thread of destiny linking Stephen Fletcher to him was for his own good, he became almost maudlin in his desire to please.

"Take the girl, then! And whatever others catch your eye. Nobody can say Yussuf is the least generous of his family!"

Marlani Chamiprak came with the girls, in transparent gauze trousers and an orange satin vest, her face dark with anger. Anklets clanked on her feet, and the thick black hair that she wore long over her shoulders, clipped here and there with silver pins, was dancing wildly, in danger of spilling loose. Fury made her walk swiftly, until she was within five feet of Yussuf Caramanli.

47

"You summoned all my girl slaves? If you need a companion for your bed this night—"

The pasha laughed even more uproariously. His hand waved at Fletcher. "They aren't for me, but for the nasrany! I'm giving him his choice of women. He has chosen the American girl. Which one is she? Bring her forward, that I may see her myself."

Marlani Chamiprak went white. She stood rigid, scarcely breathing. The *kedin* dared display no excess of emotion before the pasha, but Fletcher knew that a riptide of mad jealousy and repressed fury was sweeping through her veins.

"You heard the pasha, nasrany," she choked out. "Tell the girl to come forward. Ask her name."

Eve Doremus stepped out of the ranks of the new slave girls. She came with an easy stride, as if unaware that there were men here to feast their eyes on the smooth shapliness of her slender legs, visible through the transparent red silk trousers. The seraglio slave women had done a thorough job with her. Her fingertips were tinted red with henna. Her glossy black hair had been blued by *mesmeh* and her mouth made fuller by henna paste. A thin veil, a *khalak*, scarcely hid the thrusting firmness of her pointed breasts.

"My name is Eve Doremus," she said dully. "I'm from Boston."

There was no emotion at all in her voice. It was as if she were dead, Fletcher thought. Then he realized that she was deliberately killing any feeling inside her.

"If you can pay enough money, they'll hold you for ransom," he told her gently.

She caught the sympathy in his voice and lifted her eyes. Fletcher swore under his breath. Her little dimpled chin was trembling, and tears hung on her long black lashes. Shame and despair and an agony of spirit lay deep in those eyes. Fletcher writhed inside him at his helplessness.

Harsh laughter cut into their mood suddenly, with the bite of a whiplash. Marlani came striding forward, pointing at the woman. "She sees a fellow American. She thinks he will help her, save her from these terrible pirates. Tell her, Stefan! Tell her she belongs to you. That she is to be your own slave. A slave's slave, by Allah!"

Fletcher told her, haltingly at first, then with anger in

48

his voice as he sensed her revulsion. When he was done speaking, in the stiff military tone that betrayed his background, Eve Doremus stared blankly at him.

"You're no better than they are, are you?" she whispered. "A traitor! A renegade!"

Fletcher flushed.

Marlani Chamiprak laughed softly, triumphantly. She understood no English, but she knew contempt, in whatever language it was spoken. Back there, short minutes ago, she had been ready to kill this big blond Stefan and this woman he perferred over her. Now, she reasoned, there was a better way.

Marlani said sweetly, "Sinan, find another guard for the harem doors this night. And escort Stephen and his little American slave girl to his room. We'll have no need of him until tomorrow."

The keeper of the house nodded and salaamed. With a wave of his hand, he brought Fletcher and Eve Doremus out of the room at his heels. The chief slave, the *bash-kalfa* who had jurisdiction over the harem women at the palace, clapped his hands and followed with the slave women trailing after him.

Sinan paused in the shadow of a gallery archway. The wind moving in off the sea and past the slender columns of the arches ruffled his grey barracan, and blew a strand of brocade wall drapery across a brassbound chest of red cedarwood. The chief slave bowed to Sinan and withdrew with his barefoot girls.

Eve Doremus looked curiously at Fletcher, standing white and rigid at her side. She leaned forward and whispered in his ear, "Tonight I am going to kill myself! Or would you prefer to do it for me?"

"Don't be a stupid little fool!" he growled, and took her by an elbow.

As they moved along the corridor behind Sinan, Eve Doremus let her anger grow against this American. Strangely, she was discovering that she had no hate in her for the pasha of Tripoli or for his sea captains. They lived their lives as their forefathers had done. It was this big countryman of hers, who knew better, who seemed to be the cause of her degradation.

49

Out of the corners of her eyes, she stared at his wide chest and lean waist, naked above the copper-studded leather belt that held his scimitar on scabbard chains. With the typical yellow Moroccan leather papush on his feet, with his body, bronzed from long exposure to the sun in the stone quarries, and his thick yellow hair, long uncut, he made a barbaric figure. She could feel his strength in the fingers that gripped her arm, and sullenly she tried to wrench herself free.

He shook her a little, growling, "Behave yourself. You don't think I'm here because I want to be, do you? I was a marine lieutenant ·on the *Philadelphia* when she ran aground. For a year and a half, I've been working in the stone quarries." He drew a deep breath, then plunged on. "A lucky break put me in these clothes, and hung a scimitar by my side. I have it easy now; I don't want to go back to those quarries. And don't flatter yourself that your bodily charms made me pick you to take to the room they've given me. I only did it to save you from Yussuf Caramanli, or some kaputan he wants to please!"

At the door of the tiny bedchamber, Fletcher stepped aside to let Eve enter. Sinan glanced at him mockingly for his politeness. To the Turks and Arabs of Tripoli, a woman was only a thing to bring pleasure to a man. Occasionally, some harem favorite lifted herself above the anonymity of the other *kedins*, to command a share of authority, but mostly, courtesy was shown only to the master of the house.

"May Allah bless the night," Sinan murmured, and closed the door behind them.

Eve Doremus studied the little room with its rich but simple furniture. From the low bed, she brought her disturbing gaze to Fletcher.

"Maybe I didn't understand you correctly, down below. I thought you said I was to be your personal slave. That I was to—" Her cheeks were red, Eve Doremus realized. She bit down hard on her lower lip, then forced herself to say, "That I was to sleep with you, if you demanded it."

"That's what I said. I had to say it. I'm a slave myself. I do what they tell me to do, or they'll string me up by by thumbs and whip my back to pulp. Or worse."

50

He went and stood by the window, staring out over the white rooftops of the city, his eyes moving from mosque dome to minaret tower, then to the sloping roofs over which rainwater flowed into the large stone cisterns, providing the Tripolines with drinking water.

Savagely then, he told her of his slavery, and of his commission to guard the wife of Yussuf Caramanli like a common eunuch. He flayed himself with his words, letting her see his abasement, his shamed pride. His subservience to these corsairs was a disgrace to his name, and brought dishonor to the marine corps. His fists beat down against the stone window sill.

"But what would you have me do? Fight and die? Is that really better than being alive, with a chance for escape some dark night? Have you ever been so hungry you killed a man because he crushed a rotten melon with his foot so you couldn't eat it? That's what I did. I've quarried stone until my hands bled, and my back was so painful I almost cried when anyone touched it. Have you ever felt like that? Who are you to judge me? You—some spinster out of New York or Balitmore—"

"Boston," she whispered, and then he knew that she was crying.

She was at his elbow as he turned. Tears made channels in her cheeks, and she sobbed uncontrollably. As he opened his arms, she fell against him, burying her wet cheeks against his chest. Her arms caught and held him and she shook and trembled so violently that he had to hold her close against him to steady her.

"I've never—done what you did," she sobbed. "I—I am a spinster. A schoolteacher. I never knew what life could be like. Two aunts brought me up, and educated me at South Grammar School."

She told him about her girlhood in Boston along Sudbury Street, where she had played with other little girls, where she had walked back and forth from School Street. Her Aunt Maddy had been the plump, laughing one, her Aunt Tildy somewhat dour and suspicious—but only, she assured him, because of an unrequited love affair when she had been in her teens. Her father had been a whaling man in Nantucket. Her mother was a Boston girl, an Endicott.

51

When her mother died, two years after her father's disappearing on a sailing trip, her aunts took her into their house.

Stephen's scorn dissolved in unfamiliar waves of pity and concern as she spoke.

For three years, she had taught spelling and arithmetic at the Writing School bordering the Boston Common. Then the American consul to Rome and his wife had hired her as a private tutor to their children. She had taken ship at the Long Wharf, on a brigantine called the *Boston Lady*. Her branch of the Doremus and the Endicott families was not very wealthy, and at the time, the tutoring position had seemed something wonderful. She owned nothing, not even these thin garments that did so little to hide the sheen of her white flesh.

"I don't even have my pride any more. Or my freedom."

He said wryly, "You're lucky Mustafa reis didn't buy you. He doesn't like Americans."

Her head lifted proudly. "I'd have killed myself!"

He grimaced. "I suppose you think I should have killed myself, too, rather than play the eunuch to that pagan woman."

She smiled tremulously. "How can you think I'd be so presumptuous as to judge you? It was your bad luck to be picked for the slave market, when the *Philadelphia* ran aground. Besides, I'm a woman. You're a man, things are different with you. And I am grateful, believe me."

Her fingers caught his hand and squeezed, and her blue eyes, steady and honest, held his.

Then he told her of his escape plans, and of the Americans who gathered at Nicolo Gritti's Sign of the Olive Tree. He fostered excitement in her, so that she could share the hope in him. He felt a tenderness toward this girl, a spirit of protectiveness that made him feel like a man again. There was little enough he could do for her, except keep her for his own, safe and secure in his little room.

After a while, he noticed that her eyes were heavy and that her head was drooping. He turned her from the window, through which they had been watching the stars in the night sky while he talked, and brought her to the bed.

"Lie down," he smiled. "I'll sleep on the floor. The rug will feel like a feather bed beside the quarry stones."

She smiled tremulously, and stretched out on the cushions, her head cradled in a red satin harem pillow, staring up at him trustfully. In her Oriental finery, she seemed tiny and pathetic, like a child playing dress-up. He went and stood over her, bringing woolen barracans from the chest in the west wall, folding them over her against the cold wind coming in from the Mediterranean.

Then he stretched out on the carpets, rolled up in a striped barracan. After a long while, he slept.

Marlani Chamiprak lolled at her ease on the seraglio cushions. Her slim brown arm reached out toward a silver tray filled with sweets. Casually she munched on the tidbit while her mocking smile widened and her yellow eyes grew bright with triumph.

"I was worried a little last night, Stefan. I thought you had chosen the American woman to spite me. I would have been very, very angry with you if that had been the case."

Fletcher watched her put her fingertips to her mouth and suck the last of the powdered *sukkar* from them. She stirred her coppery body languidly, and one leg bent outward in a stretching motion. He wondered grimly what queer twist her thoughts were taking this morning, and a dim sense of foreboding came to him.

The *kedin* smiled sweetly at him. "If you had made love to her, I would have had her tortured to death. Perhaps you knew that?"

"No," he choked. "I didn't know it.".

She clapped her hands and laughed, swinging up to sit on the cushions, facing him, her bare feet close together, one slim brown leg exposed up to her rounded hip. "Now you know, Stefan, that I don't mean for you to have any other woman. It means that you and I can make a trade—the body of the American girl for your own."

He knew what she meant. If he wanted to protect Eve Doremus by hiding her out in his room, that was fine. It mattered not, a Malban fig to the *kedin*, as long as he did not touch her. Marlani would conspire in that safety with him, if he would make love to Marlani. It was as simple as that.

She was a desert woman, with a primitive, almost child-like directness. No sense of shame attached itself to her. A more civilized woman would have felt herself scorned, weeks ago, and would have taken vengeance on him. Like an animal, she was patient. Now that patience was to be rewarded. He was ready to fall into her hands like an overripe fruit from its branch.

She regarded him steadily, her ripe red mouth moist and pouting. Marlani Chamiprak savored this moment. It did not seem to her that she had waited long, for she was used to the endless intrigues of the Oriental harems.

Now she stirred and came to her feet. As Fletcher watched, she undid the sash that held her single garment and let it slide from her shoulders. Then she moved behind him and ran her fingers down his scarred back. Fletcher stood rigid. If Yussuf Caramanli found them like this, there would be no argument he could make that would save him. He felt her warm hands moving up over his sloping shoulders, and trembled as her breasts pressed against his back.

She whispered softly, "If you are afraid of the pasha, forget him. He is at Sabratha to examine some new recruits for his ship, and to see to its outfitting. He goes many times to Sabratha and Zliten, these days. He will not be back before morning."

She moved against him with a soft, crooning sound. She slid around in front of him and slipped her arms under his, clutching his shoulders. Fletcher felt the warmth and softness of her body, the strength of her hands, and looked down at her quivering lips as they parted, sensually, in triumph.

Against his chest she whispered, "Do not move. Remain the statue that you are, for just a little while longer!"

The women of the harem of Turkey and Araby were well trained in the art of exciting the senses, and Marlani Chamiprak had taken to her lessons with an avid thirst for learning, had practiced with a single-minded perfectionism.

Suddenly she cried out, and drew back, away from him.

"I give you permission, Stefan. Do not be a statue any longer!"

Slowly his hands unbuckled his swordbelt. Gripping the scabbard so that its chains would make no noise, he lowered it to the cushions. He kicked off his slippers. Then, on silent feet, he went to meet her.

CHAPTER 4

Yussuf Caramanli reined in his roan mare to glance upward at the darkening sky. His sailor's eye recognized that cloud for a thunderhead. A torrential rain would be sweeping across Fezzan northward in a little while. Any man who found himself out in that downpour would be drenched to the skin. Yussuf Caramanli could put up with discomfort when the need arose, but his business at Sabratha could await a more propitious hour.

Yussuf Pasha lifted his right arm. The little column of corsair captains and janissary agas that formed his guard of honor swung their barbs in rhythm to his cry.

"No need to ride on. The morrow is as good as today to look at raw recruits and newly fitted ships."

With silver ringbits jingling at headstalls and reins, they galloped back along the Tunis road toward Tripoli. They went past a date plantation and a score of Berber traders scurrying into ancient ruins for shelter. A Bedouin chieftain in flowing bournous, his long Arabic rifle bouncing wildly on his back, headed away from them on a swift-racing camel.

They passed through the desert gate and onto the Street of Fig Merchants. They rode more easily now, cantering by the great baths, their walls limed white, towering above little zinnia gardens.

Yussuf pasha let himself sink back against the high cantle of his Arabian saddle. The ride had been good for him. It seemed to put new life in his veins. He thought of Marlani Chamiprak and smiled. He had ignored his fiery *bash-kedin* for too long a time. When they trotted into the castle courtyard, he threw the reins to a Tirsa boy and dismounted. As he strode toward the castle, his tongue came out to caress his thin lips. There was no better time for making love than during a tropical cloudburst, with the rain lashing at the walls and the humidity of the day putting a sensual fever into a man's body.

He would send a slave to the harem, to inform Marlani that he was home. By the time he had bathed and donned perfumed garments, she would be with him. Yussuf Caramanli paused to savor the sea air with lifting lungs. Then he swung toward the closed doors of the selamlik.

His fingers closed on the ornate bronze circles that were the door handles, and pulled. The door swung inward.

On the cushions of the wide, low divan, were Marlani Chamiprak and the nasrany guardsman, Stephen Fletcher.

The five men crept through the deserted streets of Tripoli like dark wraiths, moving only in the shadows of the garden walls' that flanked the cobbled avenues. The approaching storm was blackening the afternoon, its gloomy pall cloaking the furtive swiftness with which they moved.

Yuvaz the Armless ran before them, lean body swaying in an unbalanced run. His moment of triumph was coming. Soon now, Yussuf Caramanli would die beneath the bared steel of these picked assassins who ran in single file behind him, hidden in their thick woolen barracans. Yuvaz quickened his pace. Yussuf pasha would take his corsair brig, the *Burak*, out to sea before long. He and his men must strike now, while the *Burak* was still without her sails, while Yussuf was so interested in his coming sea voyage that he would be an easy victim.

He had planned too long to fail now. He had been careful to select the proper time, and the proper men. He wanted no latecomers to the streets of Tripoli, no man come into power since Yussuf pasha wore the three horsehairs in his turban. He wanted, and chose, men who had known Yussuf's brother, the deposed Hamet, and who longed for his return. First, he had to be sure of their loyalty to Hamet. Then he made sure that they were strong, and hard of heart and muscle so they might bare their scimitars to do murder.

When he was sure of his men, he sidled up to them, under the mellow glow of brass ceiling lamps in the coffeehouses, or sat himself beside them on thick satin cushions as they stared avidly at naked dancing girls. His voice would whisper to them, reminding them of the days when Hamet sat where Yussuf ruled, suggesting the obvious advantages they might claim were they to approach Hamet, who hid now in Cairo, with the pashaship of Tripoli in their hands as an offering.

Startled faces smoothed out quickly. Narrowed eyes surveyed the coffeehouse or *trattoria*, that none might suspect why Yuvaz the Armless sat here whispering so animatedly

56

with such corsairs as Hajji reis or kaputan Ghazi ibn Said. It took time, but no one in the palace ever paid any attention to Yuvaz. What harm was there in a man without arms? And so his comings and his goings went unseen. In the shops and souks, they thought him only a beggar.

This was the time for murder, this day when the white anvil head of the thundercloud was racing overhead and big raindrops were soon to come splashing down into the cobbled streets. Yussuf pasha had ridden out to Sabratha this morning. Now he had come back, to take his castle by surprise.

Raindrops began to pelt down on the white domes and minaret of the Caramanli mosque opposite the palace as Yuvaz brought his killers off the Street of Arcades and into the long narrow corridor leading to the inner courtyard. It was in just such a dark, narrow passageway that the original Caramanli had gained his power in Tripoli by murdering the officers of the Turkish garrison, almost a hundred years ago. Now, as then, men on their way to slay carried their weapons naked in their hands.

"*Hé!*" snorted Yuvaz in the darkness of the corridor. "Yussuf did not take me by surprise, coming back so suddenly to his castle. I had planned to bring you men here at this time, to hide you until he returned at night. This way is even better! His own palace guards will not know he is home, and will not be alert to danger!"

As the rain pelted down in growing fury, they ran across the courtyard, past the flowering palms and the goldfish pool with its ornate dolphin fountain. Yuvaz jerked his chin like a finger at the stone stairway.

"Up there," he howled. "The first door to your right in the wall, after you enter the gallery. A double door of red cedarwood, with green bronze hinges shaped like the neck of a swan. Stab home for Hamet!"

For a moment he watched them leaping up the outer stair, then whirled and dove for the shelter of an arched portico as the rain deluged down in thick gray sheets.

The four assassins entered the gallery corridor from the outer stairway door on silent feet. They were lean men, wrapped to their glowing, intense eyes in thick gray barracans. Each man held a curving scimitar in his right hand. Their chests lifted and fell to the excitement that churned in them. Yuvaz had briefed them well on their run through the storm-clouded streets of Tripoli. At this time of day, when Yussuf Caramanli was not in the selamlik—and the castello thought him well on the road to Zliten at the moment—there would be only one guard along the corridor.

Now that Yussuf had returned home so unexpectedly, it would take time to summon other guards from their varied duties. During that interval, they must strike and strike fast. They knew where to find Yussuf—after these journeys he went to his private boudoir in the *seramlik*, to be welcomed back by his favorite wife with sweetmeats and coffee; and, if he were feeling especially healthy, with caresses.

The four assassins waited in the recess of a gallery door. They could hear the lone guard approaching. When he passed their hiding place, they would spring out at him with cold steel. Then they would run to bring the same sort of death to the pasha of Tripoli.

Yussuf Caramanli stood frozen in the doorway, between the opened red cedarwood doors. His eyes bulged, and his mouth opened and closed, soundlessly.

"Allah l'allah!" moaned Marlani Chamiprak, trying to rise and cover her nakedness.

Fletcher cursed softly and rolled from the woman, knowing that he was as good as a dead man, now. Then he realized that the pasha of Tripoli was not seeing them, though he seemed to be staring right at them. Yussuf Caramanli was rooted to the tiled floor of the doorway by livid fear. The harsh outcry of a man in his death throes was ringing up and down the corridor. An instant later, they heard the sudden pound of running feet.

Every pasha dreads assassination. It is the constant companion of the Moslem ruler. Every sultan, bey or pasha since the days of Mehmed Fatih, who established Turkish power at Constantinople when he took that great city on the Bosphorus two hundred and fifty years before, has walked in terror of cold steel in his back, or of a pistol fired into his face. It is the reason for the palace guards and the reason why eunuchs stand with their backs to harem doors.

The sudden rush of slippered feet over the gallery tiles, the scrape of scimitar being pulled from its scabbard, the hoarse breathing of men not used to murder and consequently almost as frightened by their daring as he was himself—Yussuf Caramanli knew what these sounds meant.

58

He gave a strangled cry and fell inward, rolling along the tiles. "Hamet's men," he babbled. "I should have killed him! I should never have let him live!"

The five captains that Yuvaz the Armless had taken six months to find came in the wide doorway with steel in their hands. Except for a naked woman and a nasrany guard, only the pasha of Tripoli was in the room. One of their number turned back at the doors to bolt them tight.

Yussuf Caramanli screamed thickly as he saw the four sea kaputans coming at him.

So intent were they on their task that they did not notice the big blond nasrany snatch up his own scimitar where it lay on a red velvet cushion near the low, round divan. The nasrany ran with bare feet on the tiles, making no sound. He went over the moaning Yussuf pasha in a leap that made him materialize before their eyes out of thin air.

Fletcher swung his scimitar in a cleaving cut that no blade ever made could have withstood. His edge caught one of the four at the throat and cut through that to the breastbone. Then he was moving away, scimitar reaching out to engage the blades that faced him. He danced as he fought, his naked feet shifting his body from defense to attack. His curving blade ran into a belly and stood out past the spine.

Only two scimitars faced him now. Fletcher yanked his steel free of the dead body that weighted it down, and ducked under a swinging blade.

He fought savagely, knowing the man at the door was turning and coming at him. Steel blades clanged harshly as they met. They scraped, where a blade warded off a molinello in tierce, with a nerve-shattering screech.

The lamplight caught at Fletcher's blued steel as he swung it high, then low. He fought as he had learned to fight with the cavalry sabres his father owned. During the American Revolution, his father had ridden with Francis Marion in his sweeps across the South. What his father knew of sabre fighting, which was considerable, he had passed on to his son. Stephen Fletcher blessed his parent more than once this afternoon, as he stamped across the tilework of the selamlik floor, his Damascus blade a living thing in his hand.

Slowly he backed before the simultaneous attack of those three scimitars. When they were near the divan, where Marlani Chamiprak knelt frozen and staring with terror, Fletcher went to the attack. He rushed his opponents, forc-

59

ing them into the spilled cushions around the divan.

One man lost his balance in the cushions and fell, arms waving wildly. Fletcher came at him with bloody blade. He sent the edge across the man's middle in a cut that went through flesh without obstacles. The man was dead before his back touched the floor tiles.

"Your freedom, nasrany," croaked Yussuf pasha. "Your freedom if you kill them! No! Take one of them alive! I want one of them alive!"

Fletcher caught the voice but made no sense of the words, for steel was ringing continually in his ears now. The assassins sensed that they stood before a blade that was more than a match for their own steel, and in their anxiety, they grew desperate. And desperate men make mistakes.

One of the killers skidded on a smear of blood. As he fell, Fletcher was there before him, stabbing downward into his chest. The man coughed once, bloodily; and fell straight down, to lie with legs twitching in his death throes.

The last man tried to bring success from certain death. He whirled on a heel and ran for the unarmed Yussuf Caramanli.

Even as the pasha of Tripoli screamed his fear, Fletcher caught the man not three feet from his victim. His red scimitar swung viciously, cutting through bone and gristle between neck and shoulder. The man cried out thickly as he fell.

There was a little silence in the room.

Stephen Fletcher looked down at the kneeling pasha, and told himself that this was the time to kill the man—now, before he recovered his habitual arrogance, before his hands could snatch up the power that his name gave him. Then he remembered Mustafa reis, and the fact that a living Yussuf Caramanli was his best protection against the fanatical Barbary captain. Besides, he told himself wryly, I'm no murderer, and this man has made no attack on my life.

"Yussuf! Yussuf!"

That was Marlani Chamiprak crying out her terror at last, running on bare legs toward her pasha, her silks tied hastily about her smooth warm skin. She lifted him to his feet. As her hands soothed him, her wide, frightened eyes asked a question of the big man with the yellow hair! *What can we do? He caught us together on the divan cushions!*

Fletcher said, "It's lucky the *kedin* saw these men, high-

60

ness. Lucky too, that she found me, to warn me, so that we could come here and hide, waiting for them."

Yussuf Caramanli discovered that, now that the danger to his person was past, his strength was flowing back into his muscles. His eyes went from the nasrany to his favorite wife. Vaguely, he remembered seeing them together on the divan when he threw open the cedarwood doors. Almost immediately, or perhaps it was in the very same instant, he had heard the sounds of the assassins as they came for him.

His eyes narrowed. "You are dressed very lightly, Marlani. Those silk things hide nothing."

There was hidden fire in Marlani Chamiprak. The nasrany had given her the clue she lacked, and so her chin lifted angrily. "Is this the thanks I get? I came swiftly from the women's quarters. Would you have had me think of modesty when your life was threatened?"

Yussuf pasha put a trembling hand to his brow. His mind still reeled in reaction to the fear that had flooded his body. A brave man on the heaving deck of his flagship, he dissolved in terror at the prospect of being attacked, unarmed by a stealthy assassin.

"No, no. Forgive my words! I am all distraught."

The woman soothed him, gesturing Fletcher to assist her as she brought the pasha to the divan. "I saw them from the grilled window of my apartment, creeping across the courtyard only seconds before you returned."

The grin on Fletcher's face encouraged her lie. Marlani Chamiprak beat her fist against her bosom, grimacing dramatically. *"Bi'llah!* What could I do, a lone woman? These men would hide in the selamlik and slay you. I ran and found the nasrany."

There was a flaw in her argument that Fletcher hastened to correct. He said swiftly, "From the wall, I saw you coming along the Street of Arcades. I knew there was no time to summon guards. Your return would coincide almost exactly with the arrival of the killers in the selamlik. The *kedin* and I arrived here only a moment before you opened the doors. We were going to hide, so that I might surprise the killers, but there was no time."

Yussuf pasha nodded silently. His voice trembled with emotion. "Allah blessed the day I refused to sell you to Mustafa reis, nasrany. For this thing you have done, I give you freedom."

61

Fletcher remembered the *Philadelphia's* men that he had met at the tavern of Nicolo Gritti. He thought also of Eve Doremus, who would be left alone if he took advantage of this offer.

There was no acting blood in Stephen Fletcher, but he bowed his head and bent his knee as humbly as any *kalfa*. "I thank the pasha, but I have no desire for freedom. My people would send me back to a ship, to fight against you, perhaps. Besides, there are certain advantages I have here that I could never hope for in America."

Yussuf Caramanli sat up, staring. "Eh? What's this? You refuse freedom?"

"I've known only kindness here, since you bought me," Fletcher said, his head still lowered.

"He means the woman you gave him," Marlani Chamiprak explained hastily. Her blood still pounded thickly in her veins. It had been a near thing, back there. If it had not been for those assassins, and the American's quick wit, the nasrany and she woud be deep in some damp, black dungeon, waiting for death and praying it would be swift.

Ah, well! To love is to take chances. There would be other days, when no rainstorm would bring Yussuf back from the duties that took him far from Tripoli. If this Americano remained at the castle, she would find a way to bring him to her side many times in the near future.

"But how can I reward you?" asked the pasha in his puzzlement.

Marlani Chamiprak leaned toward her lord and master. With her eyes fixed on Fletcher, she murmured, "Free him, but make him commander of the palace guards!"

The commander of the palace guards was second only to the pasha himself in this stone fortress. He came and went, accountable to no man or woman but Yussuf Caramanli.

"Bayazid is commander now," protested Yussuf.

"Where was Bayazid when you had need of him and his sword? Answer me that! Bayazid grows fat with loafing!" Marlani hissed in his ear.

The pasha admitted grudgingly, "He grows fat, without doubt."

"A sea voyage against the infidel would work some of that fat off," urged the *bash-kedin*, smiling above Yussuf's head at Fletcher, "Take him with you when your fleet prepares to sail! Put the Americano in his place!"

62

Mashallah! With Yussuf off on a sea voyage, and this blond Americano made commander of the guard, her days and nights would be ecstatic things! A little tremor slid down her supple back as Marlani Chamiprak closed her eyes to her own imaginings.

"Yes," said Yussuf Pasha thoughtfully. "That would be a good idea. I would be able to give Bayazid command of a ship, so as not to offend his pride, and at the same time I would honor the nasrany who saved my life. It shall be done!"

Yussuf Caramanli lifted his head and looked at his favorite wife and at the blond nasrany, his dark face giving no hint of suspicion. Uneasily, Fletcher wondered if the pasha of Tripoli was as naive as he often seemed or if the man were a better actor than either he or Marlani Chamiprak.

CHAPTER 5

The Berber girl was dancing in the Olive Tree Tavern, her brown feet pounding the flagstone floor and twisting to her intricate steps through tiny pools of spilled wine, as Fletcher came through the open door. He stood a moment, savoring the scene, smelling the heavy Turkish tobacco, its fumes laying a blue pall across the big room, listening to the tambourine that the dancing girl thudded across her knuckles as she whirled, then lifted to shake until the tiny round jingles rattled madly.

His shoulder pushed a path through the crowd of homesick Greeks and womanless Spaniards and Italians, until he reached the American table. His friends were hunched forward, staring at the girl with feverish eyes. She was a pretty thing, with slim legs bared below her whirling skirt, with only copper armlets on above her middle. A twist of chained coins was wrapped about her head, dangling down over her ears and shining in contrast to the deep brown of her hair.

Fletcher caught Nicolo Gritti by an elbow as he wedged his way through the hard-breathing men. "You'll drive them crazy, letting her dance like this! Most of these men haven't seen a woman this close for over a year!"

The Italian innkeeper grinned and winked. "Berber girls

are in town this night, effendi. More than one of them will dance here. It's a favorite place for them. The slaves are more generous with the *alaik* money than the masters with their gold. Stop worrying! Stop worrying!"

Avison looked up as Fletcher slid onto the bench beside him. His even white teeth showed in a grin, the scar on his cheek hidden in shadows cast by the overhanging lamp. His elbow dug hard into Fletcher's ribs in welcome.

"I got a nice, plump girl picked out, Lieutenant. She danced just before this one. There are lots of others coming. Pick out one and enjoy yourself!"

"No time. Listen to me!"

Avison reluctantly tore his attention from the body of the Berber girl, whose rhythmic contortions were growing more savage at every crash of her anklets.

Fletcher spoke swiftly. In the three weeks since Yussuf had made him a free man, he had prowled the narrow, twisting streets of Tripoli, studying the great double walls that ringed it in. On sunny afternoons, when the pasha went to Sabratha or to Zletin, he walked the wide white stretch of sand, staring out at the blue waters of the harbor, counting the number of corsair ships and noting their armament. Hidden by thick clumps of esparto grass, he made quick, deft sketches of the barquentines and brigs that swung at their anchor chains in the roadstead.

"I have the sketches hidden in my bed," he told Avison, whose head was tilted close to Fletcher's lips, even as his eyes again followed the convolutions of the dancing girl. "The commodore would give much to get them!"

"How can we get them to Barron?"

"There's a new slave in the palace, a Frenchman. He told me Hamet Caramanli is joining forces with an American army setting out from Cairo! It's going to come by way of Tobruk and Derna to Tripoli itself. While that army is attacking by land, the fleet will sail into the harbor and bombard the castle."

Avison turned his full attention to Fletcher. Excitedly, he leaned forward. "Go on, Steve!"

"I don't know too many details about it. Only what the Frenchman knew. My thought is this: to slip out of Tripoli some dark night and go east, toward Egypt. With any luck at all, we can contact the American forces and join up with them." He hesitated, then went on. "There's a girl in the palace, an American named Eve Doremus. We can't leave her here. She'll have to come with us."

Avison frowned. "She may not be able to keep up."

"I'll carry her, then. But I won't go without her."

"No," Avison muttered softly. "I wouldn't leave an American dog behind in this place after we break out, much less a girl! When do we go, and how?"

A great roar rose from the tables around them as the supple Berber girl bowed low, collapsing gracefully on the stone floor. Then she was gone, and in her place stood another girl.

Under cover of that animal cry, Fletcher said, "Nobody guards the desert gate that leads onto the road to Tagiura. One week from tonight, we'll meet on the road to the gate, near the cemetery. It's only a few steps from there to the gate. Before anyone sees us, we'll be gone. I'll arrange to have horses waiting for us, if I can."

"I'll tell the others and have them spread the word. We'll get everybody but Captain Bainbridge himself out of here!" said Avison.

"There's no chance of taking him?"

Avison smiled grimly. "They're holding him for ransom."

"They won't hurt him, then. All right. When I have further word, I'll come again to the tavern."

Fletcher stood up. The new Berber dancing girl was removing her skirt, and not a man noticed Fletcher as he slipped backward through the jostling crowd, to glide through the doorway and out into the street.

A black shadow moved in the moonlight, at the corner of the street. A man who had been watching the tavern doorway turned and ran with scurrying strides—a man with no arms on his body.

As Fletcher came through the narrow passageway into the palace courtyard, staring red eyes in a dark bearded face came out of the darkness at him. Fletcher put a hand to the curved dagger he wore always at his belt, in the fashion of the Moslems. The hissing voice of Yuvaz the Armless interrupted his draw.

"*Saida!* Peace between us, nasrany! I—like you—am a victim of Yussuf Caramanli!"

Fletcher studied the man, seeing the dark face and its untrimmed beard, the wild, reddened eyes that were never still

65

but glancing always from corner to corner, into those places where the shadows were blackest. The loose, pendulous lips worked continually. Furtiveness and suspicion, hate and caution lived in this man by day and by night.

"I followed you to the Olive Tree Tavern. I have followed you before. Tonight I slipped in after you, and saw you speak with the other Americanos."

"Why tell me? Don't you know I could put this blade into your heart before you could cry out? Without arms, how could you defend yourself?"

Yuvaz showed black teeth in a grin. His head came forward on hunched shoulders. "No need to kill the man who'd help you! I know a few words of your tongue. Before Yussuf deposed Hamet, I was Hamet's most trusted counselor. That's why Yussuf keeps me alive like this, to let him see how helpless his brother has become. I've become a symbol to him.

"But never mind me. It's you I want to talk about. I heard you say 'escape' and 'horses.' You can never get enough horses in Tripoli for the number of Americanos who will want to go with you."

The Marine frowned. "I'd hoped to buy them one or two at a time. But why so much interest in what I do?"

"I want to help you." The man wriggled his long body in his eagerness. "Don't you see? If I could spite Yussuf in this and free men like yourself and those other Americano sailors and marines, who might strike back at Yussuf Caramanli—hah! I'd be laying the way for Hamet to return."

Yuvaz paused, and Fletcher could see his red eyes glowing in the dark. "For my boon from Hamet, for helping you put him back on the throne, I'd ask only one thing—Yussuf himself! Yussuf, and a slave with arms and hands to do what I tell him!" Yuvaz giggled. "Can you imagine the tortures I've dreamed up for the usurper? Eh? It's all I think of, day and night—tortures and more tortures! Each day a different kind! Each night before I fall asleep, I add new twists—more subtle ways of making Yussuf suffer!"

The night wind off the Mediterannean was cold and damp. Fletcher didn't know whether he shivered from the wind or the mad words he was hearing. He said harshly, "Then you'll get me horses?"

The big head of the armless man nodded. "Horses, and food and water. Weapons, too. A sword or pistol for every

66

man, with a few rifles. And ammunition. I have friends in Tripoli. Don't think Yussuf counts every corsair captain in the city as his friend. Hamet left many good men behind him, men who would do much to see him come back. Well? Well?"

"What can I say? I'd be a fool not to take your offer."

Yuvaz stared across the majolica tiles of the courtyard. He studied the splashing fountain and the palms that swayed high overhead in the wind. As if reassured, he looked again at the American.

"We must not be seen together. You make your plans. I will have the horses and weapons for you."

The hour was late. There was no need for more words between them. Fletcher grinned and clapped a hand to the Arab's shoulder. Then he was gone in his long, loose stride, toward the stone stair that would bring him to the upper gallery.

Behind him, Yuvaz the Armless shrank back into the darker shadows. He stood a long time, motionless. His mind raced from thought to thought, balancing, rejecting. It could be done, what he promised the Americano. It would be a good way to strike at Yussuf Caramanli. He heard gossip in the taverns—there was talk that Hamet was joining forces with the Americanos. If this big nasrany were to join him with two score sailors and marines, they would help bring Yussuf down into his hands.

On the other hand, if he did not go through with his promise, but betrayed this blond Stefan Fletcher to Yussuf Pasha, he would allay any suspicions the younger Caramanli might have as to his trustworthiness. *Bi'llah!* He knew only too well that Yussuf Caramanli was turning the palace inside out to find the man or woman who let in the killers three weeks ago. If only that Americano had not interfered, or had been a little less spectacular with the scimitar!

Yuvaz sighed. A man cannot have everything.

He sidled away from the inner courtyard wall. When the torturers came to question him, if they did, he would be ready for them. He would prove his loyalty to Yussuf—and so be permitted the run of the palace as before, to scheme and connive for the deposition of the pasha—by exposing this Stefan Fletcher and his plans for escape.

Yuvaz giggled quietly. No matter what happened, he could not lose. Either Yussuf Caramanli or the Americano

67

would lose. Yuvaz preferred it would be Yussuf, but he would let the dice in the palm of destiny decide.

Eve Doremus was huddled on his little bed, wrapped in a thin grey barracan, as Fletcher came through the doorway. Lazily she turned her head and stared at him. For three weeks now she had been here when he came back to his room in the early hours of the morning. He had grown used to the sight of her, to her long, brooding silences, during which her blue eyes never left his face.

He wondered what she did while he was on duty in the seraglio, or marching beside the swaying palanquin in which Marlani Chamiprak took the air of Tripoli. Once he had looked up from the courtyard and seen her leaning against a mullion, staring out at the vast expanse of the Mediterranean. Another time he had come face to face with her suddenly in one of the underground passageways. He never asked questions; he respected her privacy, and tried to treat her as he might a sister come to visit him.

Now he sensed a new mood in her. She stretched a little, and smiled. "I'm getting fat, loafing like this, with absolutely nothing to do."

He realized that she wanted to talk, to chatter idly and at length about little things, the way she might with one of her aunts. He supposed this was her greatest need, the desire for female companionship. He sat gingerly on the edge of the low bed and smiled.

"You don't eat a thing. Except a little fruit, now and then."

She made a face and giggled. "Or some of that barley paste they call *zammita*. It tastes like my Aunt Tildy's hasty pudding. Not sweet enough, not moist enough. Always just a little bit sour."

Her blue eyes grew cloudy. "Poor Aunt Tildy! If she could see me now, she'd die of heartbreak—if she didn't die of shame first. Her Eve, slave girl to a slave!" She sighed, but there was no bitterness in her. Fletcher suspected glumly that she was enjoying her martyrdom. "Especially to such a slave!"

She smiled wanly. "Oh, I've heard the rumors about you and that woman you profess to despise. She's heels over poll in love with you, isn't she? That Taureg girl—Shellah, her name is, isn't it?—told me all about it. Seems you've

68

made some sort of deal with her, to protect me."

The first gray of dawn was seeping into the room. In its pale light, Fletcher flushed. Instantly her hand was on his wrist, gripping it tightly. Her fingers were warm and soft.

"Please," she whispered. "Please don't misunderstand me. I don't know how to put all this into words. You've no idea how long I've thought about what you're doing for me. It's just that I've always been so mixed up, but now—" She licked her dry lips and sat up. "Sometimes I want to meet that hussy in a dark passageway and go to work on her with my fingernails. Other times I want to take a stick to your shoulders. Mostly, I just cry."

She could tell he had no idea of what she was talking about, or why she was telling him all this. Amusement struggled with the momentary vexation in her. Aunt Tildy had said that men were irksome creatures, more than once.

"You're upset and worried," he soothed her.

"That's just it, I ought to be," she said dryly, "but somehow I don't feel really worried any more—not worried, only—"

How does a woman tell a man she loves him? she asked herself. Especially a woman who has been brought up most properly, in strait-laced Boston, by two maiden aunts. That wanton baggage Marlani could show off her flesh to him, but Eve must observe the rules of decorum, even if she was his slave.

And so, to take her mind off herself, she began to talk about Boston, making him see the tall ships off Long Wharf, riding at anchor as they swung to the tide swells; taking him on her walks down King Street, past the old church. She took him skating on the ponds in wintertime, but only in the early hours of the dawn, when there were few people on the ice. He sat with her for hours as she pored over her textbooks or sat fascinated with a tattered copy of Richardson's *Pamela*.

Slowly, as he listened, Fletcher realized what a lonely child Eve Doremus had been. He didn't need to hear any more about the pets she kept, or the hours she spent alone in the big kitchen, learning how to cook truffles and bake berry pastries. With this new understanding came a sudden tenderness. He put his hand on hers, and squeezed her fingers gently. The contact stirred him deeply, and he felt a warmth spread slowly inside him.

"Ships and the sea," he said slowly. "It seems they're tied up together in our lives. I used to watch the packets myself, when they came sailing up the Potomac with their sails fat and the rigging snapping so loud I could hear it up on the hill where I lay. And the Tripolines captured me off the *Philadelphia* as they took you off the *Boston Lady*."

He went on to talk of the plantation manse where he had been born. It had been a big house, with unexpected little rooms tucked under slanting roofs or below staircases. With a wooden sword that a slave carved for him out of a length of cypress shingle, he had been Captain Kidd or Blackbeard or John Paul Jones. A chair and an old walnut lowboy became his galleon or his frigate. He had two younger sisters, but they looked with scorn on his games. Loneliness had been no stranger to him.

Later, when he could sit a horse, he rode with his father across the wooded acres beyond the tobacco fields, or journeyed by post coach to the Baltimore works to stare in awed amazement as the molten metal was poured into its moulds. All that property would be his one day. By his twelfth year, it was time for him to learn what his responsibilities were to be.

He laughed a little ruefully. "There was still too much of Captain Kidd and Captain Jones in my blood, I guess. All I could think of was the sea. Despairing, my father wrote to Benjamin Stoddert, the Secretary of the Navy. He secured me a post as midshipman on the *Constellation*, under Captain Truxton."

Fletcher had begun as a midshipman, but the sea was not in his blood as much as he liked to think. When the post was offered, he snapped at a commission in the marine corps, recently re-created by an Act of Congress. Service with Truxton on the *Constellation*, including the naval fights with the *Insurgente* and the *Vengeance* during the short naval war with France; a transfer to the *Adams;* and then time on the *Philadelphia* completed his tour of duty. His service had put its brand on him, without his knowing it. His straight carriage and the efficient, unemotional manner he assumed in emergencies reflected his training as a marine officer.

Eve sighed and squirmed deeper into the cushions. For the first time in her life, she wanted to be taken into a

70

man's arms and kissed breathless, to hear him whisper that he adored her, that he needed her as a necessary part of her life. But her own training—as a ladylike young Bostonian, showed, too, and she contented herself with gripping Fletcher's hand, and staring into his eyes, as he talked until at last she fell asleep.

CHAPTER 6

The *Burak* swung lazily on her great anchor chains. Her three masts hung stripped of sails, the spars and rigging lifting like skeletal fingers from the deck, where men worked with swabs and rags to clean her planks and bulwarks against the coming voyage.

Yussuf pasha sat on a low, cushioned stool before the striped deck tent that had been raised on the quarter-deck for his own personal use. With a scimitar between his spread thighs, he leaned, forward, hands on knees, dark eyes roving the main deck, studying the rippling back muscles of the slaves polishing the brass barrels of the carronades, moving to the Kuroghler natives whose practiced hands were expertly coiling rigging ropes for storage in the bilge below.

In the days of Dragut reis and Horuk Barbarossa, the Barbary corsairs had sailed the Mediterranean in swift galleys, their oarbanks manned by chained slaves. With the coming of sailing ships, the corsairs discovered that they were outdistanced in speed and gunpower by ships built at Bristol and Marseilles. With the aid of Flemish and French shipbuilders, lured to North Africa by gold, the corsairs had answered back with barquentines and brigs that could run with any wind.

The forests of Sherdil were stripped to make towering masts and yards up to one hundred feet across to support the weight of their sails. Long low ships were turned out, fitted with twenty-four pounders or brass eighteen pounders. Brigs and brigantines, together with big, three-masted barquentines, came down off the stays to fly the star and crescent banners of the corsairs.

The *Burak* was a sleek barquentine. She lay low in the water, her lines shaped to slice the blue Mediterranean waves. More than eighty cannon of varying sizes—from the big thirty-two pounders on the lower gun deck to the carronades on the roundhouse—poked their gleaming muzzles overside.

Yussuf pasha told himself this was a good vessel. Had not a lamb been slaughtered across its prow by a holy man, to symbolize the infidel blood her men and guns would shed? The shopkeepers and *armadores* of Tripoli had hung their presents for the slaves and crewmen from yards and rigging when she first set out to scavenge the inland sea. In accordance with old custom, had not more gifts come on the launching day, and after that the feasting? Now the *Burak* was his flagship, and Yussuf Caramanli saw to it that she remained the finest and the strongest of his entire fleet.

The sun was warm overhead. It made a man drowsy, and brought to mind the comforts of the selamlik, with iced rose sherbet poured into silver goblets by pretty slave girls. The pasha stood and stretched, and beckoned his aga to his side.

"Sit you here, Jibril. Keep your eyes on the men. See that the ship is ready for departure by dawn. Work them by lamplight when it gets dark, if necessary."

The aga, who commanded the soldiers on the barquentine, nodded grimly. The *Burak* was hidden here in the shoals of this harbor off Tagiura, with a projecting spit of towering cliff sheltering her from the sea. A ship could be lighted here, and the American blockaders would be none the wiser.

"It shall be done, Highness," he promised.

Yussuf Pasha went overside and was rowed ashore in a pinnace. As he neared the stretch of white sands he saw the armless figure of Yuvaz waiting by the edge of the water. Sight of his brother's old retainer made him remember the men who had sought his life in the carpeted privacy of his palace rooms. Yussuf scowled. For a moment he wondered if Yuvaz could have been at the bottom of that little affair.

Impatient with his own imaginings, the pasha shrugged. Next he would be suspecting the infidel, Stephen Fletcher, himself!

Yuvaz came to meet him as the longboat grounded its keel in the sand. Yussuf did not enjoy the sight of the Armless One. No man really likes a constant reminder of his own ignoble deeds, but Yussuf suffered him to live because Yuvaz' helplessness symbolized the similar helplessness of Hamet, his brother.

Yussuf Caramanli scowled blackly and continued walk-

ing between the clumps of esparto grass. His stride made
Yuvaz scurry to keep pace with him.

"Well, Yuvaz?"

"A greeting, master of Tripoli. A greeting and a warning."

"Against whom?"

Yuvaz caught the sudden note of terror in the pasha's
voice. The armless man knew Yussuf would throw him to
the dungeon hooks if he suspected that he could learn anything by doing so.

So Yuvaz groveled as his knees bent. He rubbed his face
across the sandy boots of the Caramanli. "Nothing yet,
Highness. A few words I overheard the other night, spoken
by the bodyguard of the *bash-kedin,* fair Marlani herself.
He spoke with the Americano woman, Eve Doremus. He told
her he would escape from Tripoli and take her with him."

Yussuf Pasha stared down at the bent back before him.
Then with a roar of rage he lifted his heavy boot of yellow
Moroccan leather and sent it thudding hard into Yuvaz'
unprotected ribs.

"Son of a foul mother! Scum of street gutters! Now I
know your lying tongue was bred by the master of all liars,
Shaitan himself! I offered the nasrany Stefan his freedom
weeks ago. He refused it! Escape? What need has he of
escape? He can walk out by way of the desert gate or the
road to Tunis any time he wants!"

Yuvaz shuddered. He had not known of this development.
Fletcher had said nothing, being tight-lipped by nature, and
Marlani Chamiprak and Yussuf Pasha did not consider it
worthy of mention. Beads of sweat crawled out on Yuvaz'
brow as that boot slammed home against him. In his eagerness to protect himself from suspicion he had erred! He
trembled.

"Whelp of whores!" panted the pasha in his relief. He
lashed out again with his foot. "Should I have my execu-
tioners put red-hot rods in your eyes? Sharp needles to your
ears? Blind and deafen you, so that you would be less than
a mole crawling in the ground?"

"No, master! Gracious father of all pity and understanding! Forgive me!"

Yussuf Caramanli towered above the prostrate, trembling
Yuvaz. His smile was cruel as he stared downward. "Say
prayers to Allah that I leave on a sea journey, armless one!
Otherwise I would have time to take your case under con-

sideration. I might decide on the torturers, after all. You breed trouble and intrigue with your lies and false accusations! Did not the nasrany save my life, when he might have let me die? He is a man of honor, even if he is an infidel!"

Still shaking with fury, Yussuf turned and walked away, kicking up sand puffs with his yellow boots. Behind him, Yuvaz trembled uncontrollably. This had been a close one! Everything he had planned was ruined! Now the pasha would never believe him, even if he were to go to him with his story of the real escape!

"*Inshallah,*" he moaned, rubbing his face in the sand. "My tongue is a miserable traitor to my body!"

A thought came to him, and his spasmodic shiverings ceased. He knelt back on the sand, looking after Yussuf Caramanli. Slowly, his loose, thick lips twitched into a grin. There was a way to save his skin, by the black stone of Mecca! A way in which to prove his innocence and his loyalty, and thus save his flesh from the torturers. All he had to do was procure those horses for the nasrany Stefan, help him in his escape from Tripoli—then betray him at the last moment!

He would go to Yussuf Pasha when their plans were complete. The Caramanli would send a file of horsemen to the appointed meeting place, and find the Christian dogs about to flee. Hai! Praise be to Allah! Then the pasha would talk no more of torture in the same breath that he cursed the name of Yuvaz the Armless!

As he came up from the Tagiura shore, Yussuf Caramanli found his mind occupied with the thoughts stirred up by Yuvaz the Armless. It just might be the armless one spoke a little truth, mixed in with his lies, as a kitchen cook mixes in bits of salt with the barley and water. The nasrany could have refused his own freedom, so that he could take Eve Doremus with him. That sounded reasonable enough. Yussuf shrugged. Then let them go. Giving up an infidel woman was no great loss. Especially one of those proud Americanos who, if a man so much as touched her ankle, would as soon as not slip a knife into her bosom—or worse, into the ribs of the man who sought to caress her.

Let Stefan take her with him, if he wanted. It was little enough payment he could make the man, in return for saving the pasha's life.

Yussuf studied the great double walls of Tripoli. There were stones in those walls that had been there for uncounted centuries, back as far as the olden times, when the city had been called Oea by the Phoenicians who founded it, and by the Egyptians who came trading here. In those days it had joined Septis Magna and Sabrata to form the three cities, from which it took its name. Then, great catapults and mangonels had stood on the white walls, instead of brass and iron cannons.

Yussuf straightened in the saddle so abruptly that his Berber mare danced sideways, nervously. Those cannon! The infidel, Stephen Fletcher, knew where each saker stood, and the emplacement of every forty pounder! And Fletcher was a United States marine!

Let him escape, and he would bring word of those gun emplacements to the Americans! He would draw them a diagram of the castello's defenses! The nasrany was no fool. If he were to reach the American fleet after escaping from the palace, he would be worth two frigates to them!

Then Yussuf Pasha smiled and relaxed in his high Arab saddle. There was a way to prevent the American from leaving Tripoli and taking his mine of information with him.

Marlani Chamiprak stalked back and forth in the selamlik, her nostrils flaring with anger as her voice grew shrill and grating. Clad in loose muslin trousers, she stalked around the room, waving her slim bare arms indignantly.

"On a sea trip? Me, your *bash-kedin?* I never heard of such a thing!"

"It is a rare occurrence," admitted Yussuf wryly. "Still, it has been done before, by kaputans and reis madly in love with a wife or with a slave woman."

He lay relaxed on the great wide divan, loosely clothed against the heat, his dark eyes following Marlani. He enjoyed these displays of temper in his favorite, for as anger flamed in her, calmness grew in him.

"I've told you my reasons. It is suspected that the nasrany means to flee with the Americano girl."

"You heard him reject your offer of freedom!"

"True words. But it just could be that he's acting a part, to kill any suspicions we might have of him."

She shrugged contemptuously. "You give him credit for being a very kadi for subtlety!"

"I take no chances. But to demonstrate that I am as subtle as he, I'm going to take you with me. He will go along as your bodyguard. You will take the American woman as your body servant, so you can keep your eye on her, to make sure she plans no treachery. Mustafa reis will come too, as second in command. He will make certain, never fear, that Stefan Fletcher will play no tricks on us!"

"The whole thing is ridiculous," she said flatly. "I'll die of suffocation, cooped up in the deck tent."

Yussuf laughed. "The salt air will be good for you. You'll have all the roundhouse deck to stroll."

"I may be killed! I suppose you would like that?"

"All I plan to attack are merchantmen!"

"And the Americano fleet? What are you supposing they will do when you come sailing out onto the inland sea?"

His hand gestured lazily. "I do not fear them. They have big ships. I have fast ones. I will outrun them if they sight us."

Marlani Chamiprak relaxed slowly, as the thought came to her that she would have the big blond nasrany at her side during the coming voyage. It might have been worse. Yussuf could have left him behind, in one of the dark dungeons with a chain fastened to his ankle. As it was, she would have him always beside her, to lessen the monotony of the sea journey. Her heart thudded excitedly as she wondered if she would have a chance, in the shelter or the deck tent, to savor the American's kisses. It would add a flavor to them, knowing that Yussuf was on the ship and that if he saw them together, he would make them die an especially horrible death.

Eve Doremus was fretful. For the fifth time in the last ten minutes, she stared at her reflection in the ancient mirror of polished silver hanging on the wall of the little room. Her glossy black hair hung loose and long, spilling across her naked shoulders and down her back. A thin golden fillet was thrust into her hair, a jewelled pendant dangling low on her forehead.

She wore a jacket and clinging trousers of black lace, through which her white skin showed like snow dappled with dark shadows. The *kalfa* girls had rubbed perfume, sweet and heady, into her hair and over her flesh. A dozen golden necklaces hung between her high, firmly molded breasts. Her feet were bare, but her toes had been tinted as red as her fingernails.

A thick flood of hunger enveloped her, filling her with a pleasant excitement. She could not even sit down with this restlessness working in her veins. She held her palms flat to her flushing cheeks, and tried not to think what her aunts in Boston would say if they could see her now. But strangely enough, she felt no shame.

She was no longer an austere New Englander, but a slave girl in a barbary harem, Eve tossed her head, haughtily. A slave girl! Well, then! She would behave like one. The morals that might have done for Boston had no place here. For more than three weeks now, she had shared this room with Stephen Fletcher. Night after night, she had lain sleepless as he crept in to roll up in a barracan on the floor. More than once she had been tempted to reach out and beckon him to the low couch where she lay alone.

Eve turned a little, hands on hips, regarding her reflection. She thought she had never looked so attractive. Surely she was just as tempting to the big marine as that desert hellcat, Marlani Chamiprak! Blushing furiously, she shrugged back the black lace jacket so that it hung from her elbows, revealing the fullness of her bared white breasts. Was a brown African woman more desirable?

She was so lost in herself that she didn't hear the door latch lift or the door swing inward. Fletcher stood there, staring at her reflection in the mirror. For long moments they gazed at each other in the polished silver. Feeling the blood rising from her throat to her cheeks, Eve slowly shrugged the lace vest up over her shoulders. Fletcher's shining eyes, full of worship and desire, told her all she wanted to know.

She moved toward the low bed, her heart pounding madly, knowing that if he came toward her now, she would turn and fling herself into his arms, as wild as any dark-skinned harem girl!

"Eve!"

That choked cry held her motionless. She heard him run across the room to her; her skin was afire where he touched her to clasp her hard against him. Her eyes closed tight, and her lips parted as she leaned her head back against his shoulder.

77

"Stephen, I—I'm shameless! I don't know—what's come over me!"

"Don't talk! Not now!"

He turned her slowly and Eve felt the world spinning under her bare feet. Then the breath was going out of her as his strong, hard arms locked her in against him and his lips were on hers, drawing the life from her and replacing it with a sweet white flame that burned and burned.

When his mouth left hers to caress her throat, she uttered wordless sounds, smiling faintly, rubbing her chin against his cheek. Laughing softly, she tilted her face away from him and whispered, "Am I as lovely as Marlani? Do you want me as much as you want her?"

His only reply was to crush her to him again, his mouth once again seeking hers. All the while her body was being slowly transformed into a bright, living flame. Then, suddenly, she was being lifted and carried across the room and, finally, lowered to cool silken cushions.

"Stephen," she whispered imploringly as she drew him warmly beside her.

CHAPTER 7

The corsair ship ran through the blue waters of the Mediterranean with her taut sails humming, mainstays whipping in the offshore breeze. The sky was a blue emptiness overhead, and the sun made a yellow haze through which the brig slipped with the ease of a gull riding an air current. Stephen Fletcher stood with his hip to the quarter-deck rail, discovering again the heady fragrance of salt air and sea spray. He was re-discovering his sea legs, too, swaying with the faint swing of the brig as the blue swells lifted it.

Behind him, in a low chaise set before the striped magnificence of the deck tent, Marlani Chamiprak watched him. Beside her knelt Eve Doremus, her strong white fingers braiding the thick black hair of the pasha's favorite wife. Occasionally Marlani cried out against the pain of a tormented scalp, as a strand of hair was twisted with extra vigor.

"Be careful, *kalfa!*" rasped Marlani Chamiprak, after a particularly vengeful tug. "Hurt me once more, and I'll have you whipped naked at the big mast yonder!"

Eve murmured softly, "It isn't my fault. The ship pitches so steeply. I lose my balance."

"Be more like your countryman, then. See how easily he stands, no matter what the ship does." Glancing slyly at the girl, she added, "In your weeks of living with him, you must have found him very entertaining. What kind of lover is he?"

"Why ask me?" Eve whispered hotly, feeling the sting of jealousy inside her. "Your eyes would never burn so brightly if he was nothing more than bodyguard to you!"

Marlani choked in her anger, twisting sideways on the cushioned divan. The white kitten on her lap stirred restlessly, lifting its little head and spitting.

"You nasrany slut! I will have you lashed!"

Eve lowered her head until her long black hair veiled her face. "You will have to give the pasha a reason. Will you tell him I am jealous of you? That I love the nasrany? That you want him for yourself?"

The *bash-kedin* pulled her hair free of Eve's fingers. Petulantly, she lay back among her satin pillows. "I will find a way to make you pay, yet. See Mustafa reis yonder, by the rail. See how he keeps staring at your precious Stefan. How would you like me to talk Yussuf into giving you to him, eh? He does not like Americans. He would enjoy torturing such a pretty American as yourself."

Eve shivered. This woman, whose person she was forced to attend, was not only the woman who stood between Stephen and herself. She was the woman whose power in Tripoli was as great as that of Yussuf Caramanli for she ruled the pasha. In hurt pride and jealousy, Eve's tongue had run away with itself. Her white back, exposed now to the warm Mediterranean sun, had never know the sting of a whip. But she had seen the scars criss-crossing Stephen's back, and had been sick with pity for him. She would be sick with more than pity if Marlani gave her to Mustafa reis.

And so she whispered, submissively, "Forgive me, Highness."

Marlani smiled wickedly, her yellow cat eyes studying the kneeling girl. "Or would it be better to give your Stefan to Mustafa reis—after I tire of him?"

The *bash-kedin* did not miss Eve's involuntary start. Her mocking laughter trailed out across the quarter-deck.

Sensually, she writhed deeper into the cushions. "Do up my hair as before, American. But be sure that you do not cause me any more pain."

A voice shouted hoarsely from the maintop, where a Musselman sailor stood leaning against the roperail, pointing westward toward à big merchantman rolling with the waves.

"*Balak! Balak!*" he screamed.

At the sound of that wild cry, men in turbanned helmets and coats of mail under their white jelabs ran to the ratlines, carrying rifles and pouches of bullets. These were the sharpshooters who hooked trousered legs in the rigging and poured their fire across the decks of enemy ships. Men with only twists of cloth about their loins scampered up the companionways to the gun deck, where big thirty pounders awaited their hands at tampions and spring locks. On the main deck itself, the carronades were serviced by gun crews and young boys, the powder monkeys who brought up the gunpowder in black silk bags.

Fletcher came across the quarter-deck at the wave of Marlani Chamiprak's hand. She stood with the wind pressing her thin shawl against her body, her dark eyes alight with excitement. Fletcher smothered his smile at the sight of Eve Doremus glowering at her.

"Will there be fighting, Stefan?"

"She's a merchant ship. Spanish, from the cut of her hull. Big and slow. Not many cannon. It'll be mostly cut and slash with swords on her deck."

Yussuf Pasha came leaping up the stair, unbuckling his belt and scabbard. He would lead his men with his scimitar in hand, no scabbard to encumber him.

"A rich prize, nasrany. She is homeward bound from Italy."

They could see the big merchantman floundering awkwardly in the sea swell as her captain attempted to turn her with the wind and race the fast corsair ship toward a safe port at Malta. The wind caught her big courses and sent her careening into a wave. The wave shook her, turned her half around. She lost headway, wallowing in a trough. Her sails flapped loosely.

Yussuf shouted his exultation at the sight.

"She as good as invites us to come aboard. See how she shudders to the waves. Her captain will be some time right-ing her. When he does, we'll be on him!"

The pasha put an arm about Marlani Chamiprak and drew her in against him. "I'd intended to order you below, most favored one! Instead, I'll let you stand and watch how I make my sea captures! Guard her well, Stefan. If danger threatens, put her below!"

The *Burak* ran after the floundering schooner with the grace of a greyhound streaking for a clumsy sow. With the wind aft, she came down to starboard, gun muzzles gleaming from her open gunports. A shout lifted from the brown throats of the Tripoli raiders at rigging and main deck as soon as they could see the merchantman's guns.

"Only two cannon at her stern, and three to either side," muttered Fletcher. "She's not been scraped in a long time, either. She's as hard to handle as an untamed stallion."

"What will Yussuf do?" asked Marlani, standing on tiptoes to peer across the blue stretch of tossing waters at the clumsy vessel.

"Put a shot across her bow, probably. No sense in sinking her, when she's helpless to his will."

Eve Doremus came to his right side, and her warm little hand crept into his palm. "There are women on board," she whispered.

Fletcher could see them, being hurried below decks. They would be grist for the slave market in the great square. He felt a spate of red rage run through him. These corsairs had ruled the Mediterranean since the days of Khair ed Din in the early sixteenth century; they had gained their reputation over several hundred years of plundering. They had been and still were fierce fighting men. The irony of it was that the Barbary fleet was a relatively small one. And yet the western nations preferred to pay tribute, rather than organize a powerful fighting fleet that could blow the corsairs out of the waters and put an end to their ravages. And as long as this shocking state of affairs existed, neither men nor women could sail the Mediterranean safely. Gentlewomen like the Spanish senoras in the ship across the water from them now, girls like Eve Doremus, and Italian and French noblewomen unlucky enough to fall into the corsairs' hands, would be sold at slave marts like the Place of Miracles in Marrakesh, or the trading blocks at Algiers and Morocco.

The distance between the *Burak* and the merchantman

81

had lessened to a hundred feet. Yussuf Caramanli stood on the lower deck, ringed about by his raiders in turbanned helmets and chainmail. His scimitar flashed high in the sunlight as he waved it to the deep shouts of his eager janissaries. On the far flank of the boarding party was Mustafa reis, his thin lips stretched in a tight smile, his long black topknot seeming to dance in eagerness where the sea breeze caught it.

Grapnels were being dangled by sailors in the ratlines, about to be hurled. A wave lifted the *Burak* and took her closer. Now the sailors in the ropes whirled the grapnels and sent them slipping through the air, to dig pointed flukes deep into the deckwood of the merchantman. Muscles bulged on their backs and arms as the two ships were tugged together.

"*Allahu Akbar! Allahu Akbar!*"

"*Inshallah! God is great!*"

Their cries came up to the quarter-deck as the corsairs milled restlessly below, leaning from rails and shrouds to shout their battle cries down at the pitifully few soldiers drawn up to receive them.

"It'll be over in minutes," said Fletcher heavily.

Yussuf Caramanli leaped the few feet separating the *Burak* from the Spanish ship. His men came after him in a surge of flashing steel and throaty screams. They jumped like frogs deserting a rock at the approach of a snake. Bare feet and sandals clung to the merchantman's deckboards as the marauders recovered balance.

Then Yussuf pasha led them at the Spaniards, who stood surprisingly calm, with their rifles raised, unruffled and undismayed. In another mood, Yussuf Caramanli would have been suspicious, but now the heat of easy victory was in him with a numbing sweetness. All he could think of was the profit this ship would hold, the strong slaves he would capture.

Just as the two lines crashed together, the Spanish rifles spurting lead and flame, a roar went up from below decks. The pasha whirled and cursed.

Up from the twin companionways of the merchantman came a horde of men in the trim green and white uniform of Spain. They carried rifles and swords, and they were led by officers with swords and long-barreled pistols.

Yussuf Caramanli had walked into a trap.

A ragged volley by the first of those silent men dropped half a dozen corsairs. An officer roared his commands, and now a hundred rifles belched their flame.

Yussuf Caramanli fell in the wave of lead that struck his men. A bald Arab hooked him under an arm and helped him to his feet.

"Reload!" screamed a Spanish officer.

Yussuf Caramanli ran for his ship, falling to the deck as he leaped over its side. Half his men lay groaning on the deck of the Spanish merchantman.

"Cast off!" he screeched.

Daggers flashed in the sun, severing the grapnel ropes. On his knees, Yussuf screamed thickly to the sailors in the rigging, to the gunners at the carronades.

"Crowd on sail! Sail! You gunners—load and fire!"

It was too late. The two ships were still fastened by a few grapnels, and the yelling Spanish soldiery swarmed onto the slim Barbary ship. Swords flashed, and here and there a pistol barked. Fighting savagely, the Spaniards drove the corsairs back.

A dozen Spaniards came for the quarter-deck, where Fletcher stood with Marlani Chamiprak and Eve Doremus. Behind the deck tent was the helm. If they could control the helm, the Spaniards would take the ship.

Sensing rescue, Fletcher drew Eve Doremus and Marlani Chamiprak to one side, against the starboard rail. He gave the Spaniards room to pass, but they were not content with this. With swords naked in their hands, they came at him, seeing in this bronzed half-naked giant only one more corsair.

His scimitar came out in answer to their challenge. Steel met and clanged as he fended off their blades. He shouted at them in English, "I'm no pirate. I'm an American!" Either they did not understand him, or chose not to do so. In the heat of battle, men forget the niceties. They swore hotly at him in fluid Castilian, and the points of their blades came thrusting at his flesh.

Eve Doremus screamed, "Don't kill him. He isn't one of them!"

She leaped forward in her anxiety, and a grinning officer fended her off with the back of a hand on her face. He shouted, "Time for you later, white one! Right now we've work to do!"

83

Fletcher saw the blow. And in a fraction of a second the realization of his feeling for Eve Doremus struck him full force, sure and true. The officer had struck the woman he loved.

Fletcher came in on the attack, two long steps at a time, his scimitar weaving high, then low. The edge caught a soldier at the neck and dropped him. The point took another in the ribs. The edge came down into the officer's face, sheering away a cheek. Screaming harshly, the officer clapped both hands to his face and fell against the rail.

Marlani Chamiprak was on the man in a moment, a slim poniard in her upraised fist. She thrust the weapon deep into the officer's throat, stabbing him again and again, screaming shrilly all the time.

The Spanish soldiers were falling back before Fletcher's attack. They were not cavalrymen, who were used to this play of steel on steel. They were riflemen, who carried swords only on rare occasion.

Fletcher's blade lifted and fell. He cut and hacked, trying to avoid more blood, seeking only to drive them to the deck stair, where he could hold them off almost indefinitely.

On the main deck, Yussuf pasha had rallied his corsairs. He pointed his bloody blade at the raised deck where Fletcher fought, and his roaring voice brought a flush of shame to his men.

"Will you let a nasrany teach us how to fight? See what he does, alone against so many! See how the infidel defends my women! Can we do less for the ship itself?"

The corsairs came raging across the deck, scimitars stabbing and hacking, dark faces were distorted by screaming. *"Halaout buòy! Halaout buòy!"*

They split the Spanish ranks in front of them, turned them and drove them back against the port rail. Scimitar blades flashed, jelabs flowed and mail sparkled. Here and there men went down with blood spreading on white uniform facings or Moslem sashbelts. A man screamed thickly in the scuppers against the agony of a severed hand. A dark Moor lay huddled near him, motionless.

The Spaniards fell back before the mad fury of the corsairs. In small groups they retreated to their decks where officers organized them into little bands of riflemen. At shouted orders, they poured their leaden hail across the Tripoline's decks.

Suddenly a huge wave lifted the two ships and tore them apart. A freshening wind filled the flapping sails of the corsair ship, and pushed it northward. As a stretch of blue water grew wider between the hulls, Yussuf Caramanli turned from the rail toward the quarter-deck.

He took three steps and fell, face down.

Staring at the crumpled body, Fletcher felt dismay and despair. Striding forward toward his fallen pasha came Mustafa reis. There was a spray of blood across his bare chest, where a Spanish officer had fallen against him as he died, and drops of blood on his cheeks and legs. He came to a stop above Yussuf Caramanli and lifted his hot, black eyes to the American man and woman on the quarter-deck. Wild triumph blazed in those fierce dark eyes.

Soon now, Stephen Fletcher and Eve Doremus would belong to him. Soon he would glut the madness in him. For when Yussuf Caramanli died, Mustafa reis would become the pasha of Tripoli!

CHAPTER 8

Mustafa reis stared up from the main deck at Stephen Fletcher. An eternity of torture and agony for the two Americans lay in those hard black eyes. The corsair sea captain let his gaze rove the girl for a long moment, before he turned and barked orders at the staring crew.

The Spanish merchantman and the corsair brig were drifting farther and farther apart. There was no fight left in either ship, for Mustafa reis wanted only to consolidate his grip on the power this moment was giving him, and the Spaniards desired nothing so much as to run and lick their wounds in peace.

"Take him to the deck tent," shouted Mustafa reis, waving a mailed arm. "Now that Yussuf is dying, I am pasha in Tripoli and on the *Burka*."

Corsair fighting men ran to do his bidding. Their strong brown hands lifted the motionless body of their former ruler and carried him gently up the quarter-deck stairs. They brought him in under the striped length of canvas and lowered him on Marlani's chaise. Mustafa reis came after them, a hand on his scimitar hilt, his chest rising and falling with excitement.

"Yussuf will be dead by sundown," he announced, staring into the bloodless face of his pasha. "I will rule in Tripoli and on the Mediterranean! His palace will be my palace, his women, my women. His slaves too, will belong to me."

His hand gestured, but he did not look at Fletcher.

"Take the nasrany man. The woman, too. Chain them a yard from each other in the hold, down where the rats grow hungry."

Eve screamed and fought against the hands that caught her arms and wrists. "Not the rats, no, no! I—I couldn't stand them!"

Fletcher was surrounded by pirates, hanging about his neck, weighting down his arms. All he could do was writhe and strain, while a bare forearm against his throat choked until his head felt like an overblown balloon. Eve was dragged from his side toward the deck companionway, where all the crew and the janissaries were gathering to stare.

Then Yussuf Caramanli groaned.

The men holding Eve Doremus and Fletcher turned to look at their pasha on the lounge. A trickle of spittle ran down his jaw from a corner of his lips. Blood rose in his face, making it swarthier that usual. The blood at his ribs, where a Spanish bullet had ripped the flesh, was bright and red.

Her fear of a few moments earlier replaced by a new arrogance, Marlani Chamiprak came striding forward from the deckrail against which she had been cowering.

"The pasha is not dead," she said hoarsely, glaring at Mustafa reis. "Yussuf Caramanli still lives, and I am his *bash-kedin*. Release the Americano man and woman. They belong to me, not to Mustafa reis!"

The men stared from the angry woman to the reis. Each of them knew that, if they disobeyed Marlani Chamiprak and Yussuf Caramanli lived, they would be boiled alive in oil for their treachery. On the other hand, if they disobeyed Mustafa reis and Yussuf died, it would be the sea captain who would give orders for their death by torture. Sweat stood out on their dark foreheads, and foreboding lay in their eyes as they glanced unhappily from the *bash-kedin* to the corsair lord.

Mustafa reis was thinking hard. Yussuf was alive, but

no man could tell how long he would stay alive. Now that the pashaship was so close, he could wait a little while, and pretend loyalty, knowing that he would soon find a way to put Yussuf Caramanli in a Moslem grave.

His glance touched Marlani Chamiprak and ran down the smooth, coppery body, scarcely hidden by that silken veil. He sighed as he studied her slim legs, rounded hips and overripe breasts. He ached to taste her desert savagery on the seraglio cushions, he admitted to himself, but patience was the weapon of a clever man. Believing himself clever, he would practice patience.

The corsair captain bowed low. "The *bash-kedin* speaks truth. Our pasha is still alive, and we must do all we can to keep him alive. Release the Americanos. Give them to her command, so that they can nurse our pasha."

Hands fell away from Fletcher as grateful sighs reached his ears.

Marlani Chamiprak clapped her hands. "Bring hot water and clean cloths. Hurry! Hurry!" She looked at Fletcher. "You have some knowledge of wounds, nasrany. As an American marine, you'll have stopped a wound before now!"

No seaman in this day and age was without some crude knowledge of emergency surgery. More than once, on board the *Adams* or the *Constellation*, Fletcher had attended to a bullet-probing during the short sea war with France.

"I'll need a thin stiletto," he told the woman.

Marlani looked at Eve Doremus. "You'll stay with me, girl, to nurse Yussuf back to health. There will be more reward in this for you than for any crewman. By keeping Yussuf alive, you'll keep yourselves alive. We three have more to lose if the pasha dies than any other."

Fletcher found a thin Italian dagger whose needle-like blade was to his liking. He knelt over the inert form of the pasha. Eve cut away the leather tunic and Marlani lifted off the coat of chainmail, baring the corpulent chest. The wound was deep and ugly. Clenching his teeth, Fletcher bent forward and began to probe.

When the pasha showed signs of recovering consciousness, Marlani held a vial of strong French brandy to his lips, forcing him to swallow. Her breathing was shallow and frightened. The thought came to Fletcher that by turning chirurgeon, he was giving Mustafa reis a chance to blame him for Yussuf's death; for if he failed in his task, that

87

wily sea captain would call him a murderer. But what could he lose, since Mustafa meant to kill him by torture, anyhow. Grimly, he worked on, his hands bathed in blood.

It took a little less than an hour, but when he was done, the leaden pellet lay on a low tea table, and clean white bandages swathed the pasha's naked chest. Yussuf was breathing hoarsely and heavily. A veil of perspiration beaded from his brown forehead, but that might only be the effect of the strong French brandy that his *bash-kedin* had poured so enthusiastically down his gullet.

Marlani came close to Fletcher, warm fingers touching his shoulder.

"Will he live, Stefan?"

"Who knows?"

Her eyes were bright, almost feverish, as she stared down at him. She breathed faster as she bent and placed her moist mouth to his. Against his lips she whispered, "If he dies, then you die, too—and I become one of Mustafa reis' harem women!"

Marlani was aflame with the excitement of this new danger. Hungrily, she pressed against Fletcher, her mouth grinding against his. He thrust her away from him roughly. The pasha of Tripoli was watching them.

Yussuf Caramanli lay with his eyes wide open, staring at his favorite wife. For an instant, before he saw Fletcher watching him, hate and fury gleamed deep in those black orbs. Then the eyelids fell heavily, and the pasha slept.

Fletcher shivered. He would not know for hours, perhaps not even until dawn, whether Yussuf Caramanli would live or die. Judging from the anger he had seen in those fierce eyes, it would make little difference to him. Mustafa reis would kill him by torture, but so might Yussuf, now that he had seen him in the passionate embrace of Marlani Chamiprak.

The *Burak* slid through the blue waters of the Mediterranean with the ease of a playful dolphin. Her rigging hummed faintly in the onshore breeze, and the sails overhead were fat with wind. Men lounged on the foredeck or worked lazily at coiling grapnel ropes. A few janissaries, under the watchful eye of the aga, mended bullet-torn mail shirts, or sharpened curved scimitars. The decks were neat and clean, and from the striped deck tent to the trail boards, the *Burak* glistened with seaworthiness.

An air of waiting held the ship and its men. Eyes that worried over a pumice stone, or a loose link in a chain-mail shirt, turned thoughtfully toward the raised quarter-deck, where the two Americanos could be seen leaning against the starboard rail. All last night those two and Marlani Chamiprak had worked to keep Yussuf Caramanli alive. He was still alive, but for how long? Dark heads shook uncertainly at this question, and dark eyes stared broodingly at Mustafa ·reis.

The sea captain squatted languidly beside a stout carron-ade. He gave no outward sign that he seethed with fury. All last night Yussuf Caramanli had hovered between life and a burial at sea. It was five hours past dawn, and he seemed stronger with every minute. Mustafa mulled over several plans in his mind, and decided finally to let the fate that Mohammed said was written in the mind of Allah guide his course of action.

Marlani Chamiprak sat on a plump hassock beside the cushioned divan where Yussuf Caramanli lay breathing heavily. Her brown hand clasped his as her kohl-shadowed eyes studied his bland, expressionless features with the de-votion of a religious fanatic. There was no hunger in this coppery woman to bed down with Mustafa reis. She had seen his cruelty often enough to know that it was an in-grained part of the man, like the flow of blood in his veins. What he had done with other women, once he tired of them, he would do with her.

Yussuf Pasha she could control. Mustafa reis would con-trol her.

And so Marlani Chamiprak, even as Eve Doremus and Stephen Fletcher, prayed to her gods that this man would live to a fine old age.

Stephen Fletcher was tired. All night he had been on his knees beside the dying man, changing his bandages, and soothing his fevered face with cold compresses. He had found a little catnip in a ship's locker, and made a hot brew to let the pasha sleep more soundly. His face was haggard, and his sunken eyes were ringed with black shadows of fatigue.

Eve stirred beside him, her white hand clutching his arm convulsively. "Will he live, Stephen? Will he?"

He shrugged. "All the ship waits for that answer. Perhaps all the world, too. Who knows what treaties Mustafa reis may sign with the bey of Algiers and the bey of Tunis? If the Barbary states unite, can the United States win out against them?"

She shivered and pressed closer, so that he could reassure her by the strength of his arm about her waist. "I'm frightened." she told him.

"Aye," he nodded. "My stomach is none too firm itself, at the moment."

Marlani Chamiprak cried out, and Fletcher whirled.

He saw her half standing, crouched forward, fists clenched at her side. He groaned, "The man's dying!" and ran into deck tent.

Yussuf Caramanli was staring upward with wide eyes. He smiled faintly.

Marlani whispered, "He lives! He lives! The fever is gone, and he knows me!"

Eve leaned heavily against Fletcher, her hands clutching his arms for balance. She moaned, "I thought—I thought it was his end, instead!"

Fletcher slid to a knee beside the lounge and with gentle fingers, sought the bandages. He laid them back as his practiced eyes studied the clean brown flesh on either side of the wound. The discoloration and swelling were gone. Unless a complication developed, Yussuf pasha would be a well man within a few days.

Across the figure of the pasha, Marlani Chamiprak lifted her head and stared at him; triumph shining in her eyes.

Yussuf Pasha lifted a hand to touch his wife. "I was at the gates of paradise, but you brought me back. I could hear the singing of the houris that Allah promises to all true believers, but just as my hands were reaching for the jeweled handles of the garden gates, I heard you calling me."

Marlani hissed into his ear, "Mustafa reis had all but made himself pasha in your place! The Americano man and woman he ordered chained in the hold! Myself he thought to enjoy on the cushions where you lie now!"

Yussuf Caramanli smiled, but his eyes darkened in anger.

The *bash-kedin* whispered hoarsely, "He would have wrapped you in a canvas shroud and tossed you over the ship's rail if Stefan had not hunted out the bullet in your ribs and doctored your flesh with alcohol.

Then, remembering the pasha's face when he had touched consciousness earlier, Fletcher added, "When Marlani saw

90

you lived, her joy was so great she couldn't restrain herself from a kiss of gratitude!"

"I owe you my life twice, then! It was a good day that Allah brought you to me, Americano! I mind I said once that the lines of our fates were interwoven, yours and mine. At the time I asked myself, for good or for evil? Now I know the answer to my question. Even the kiss helped me to regain my health, by rousing my spirit!"

His weak hand fumbled a moment at his chest, finding the snake-like chain of fine golden links holding a jeweled crescent. "Take this, Stefan. Put it about your neck. It is my gift to you, and will make you a wealthy man, for the diamonds in it alone will buy you anything from a fine ship to a harem full of women."

"Later," said Fletcher. "I don't want you to move, for now. You need rest and sleep. In a few days, you'll have your old strength back."

The pasha looked beyond Fletcher. When the American turned, he realized that Mustafa reis had come among them while they talked, and he stood now, tall and brown and silent in his chainmail and his wide trousers and pointed slippers, staring down at his ruler with enigmatic eyes.

Mustafa reis looked out across the cold waters of the inland sea, where the moonlight was tipping the waves with white fire. For five hours he had leaned against the larboard rail-capping, motionless. It was night now, and the *Burak* still fled from the wind like a hare before the hounds. Ever since mealtime, when he had spurned the rice and meat cakes the ship's cook brought him in his cabin, he had been silent and morose, roving the ship from quarter-deck to curving beak. Turmoil bubbled inside him.

Yussuf pasha lived, and would continue to live.

Stephen Fletcher and the Americano woman were safe from his torturers, as Marlani Chamiprak was safe from the seraglio cushions where he had already, in his fertile imagination, enjoyed her lush body.

And what would happen to Mustafa reis, who had dared to lift his eyes to the pashaship while the Caramanli still lived? The corsair captain shivered, and wrapped his black wool cloak tighter about his shoulders. If Tripoli were not engaged in war, Yussuf would have him hung naked in a steel cage above the market square, to starve slowly while the vultures came flying to peck away at his living body.

For the first time in his life, Mustafa reis felt gratitude toward these accursed Americanos whose big frigates could smash a brig like the *Burak* with two good broadsides. The Caramanli dared not kill him—his seamanship and his fighting prowess were needed too much for him to be put to death as a traitor. Yussuf Pasha would forget Mustafa's treason in order to protect his crown.

Ah, but when this war was over? What would happen then to Mustafa reis? Yussuf Pasha was a jealous man. He was more jealous of his throne than of his wife. With his wealth, he could buy a dozen fine wives any day in the week, but a kingdom like Tripoli came into a man's hands only once in a lifetime. No, the pasha would not forget Mustafa reis then, when peace lay across Tripoli like a marabout's blessing. That would be the time to put the rebellious reis in a cage and give him to the beaks of the vultures.

Mustafa reis smiled thinly as his brown hand closed to a fist. "I'd be a fool to stay and let him kill me," he whispered into the scarf at his throat.

Still, by leaving Tripoli he would be giving up everything it had taken years to amass, by plunder and piracy, in his great stone house near the Street of the Sailmakers. There was a better way to protect himself than this.

Yussuf Caramanli could still die, by poison.

Some minutes after dawn, a curving dagger was plunged into the back of the ship's cook. The man gurgled once, and his writhing body shuddered again and again, while Mustafa reis hammered home the length of his bared blade into the man's back.

As the cook slipped to the dirty planking of his little cookroom, Mustafa reis stepped over him to the wooden shelf where a bowl of barley porridge lay beside a tray of Balban figs. This was the pasha's breakfast. From a pocket of his jellaby, the corsair captain drew out a small vial of purple Venetian glass. Unstoppering the vial, he held it over the bowl and watched the colorless poison run down into the porridge.

Mustafa reis stoppered the flask and went to the small kitchen locker. He pushed open the locker door and placed the empty vial carefully inside where it could be easily found. Then he turned and stared at the dead cook.

Iskander could not be found dead like this, stabbed in the back. He would have to go overboard into the sea. The deck above was silent; the ship slept. Only the helmsman at the wheel and the lookout in the maintop would be awake to what Mustafa reis did in the dawn hours.

The corsair captain bent and shouldered the body of the dead cook. He was a light man, thin and bony. He wore only a thin loincloth against the heat of his cooking fires, glowing redly now in the iron braziers. Mustafa reis carried the dead cook up the companionway to the maindeck hatch and lowered him slowly to the stairtreads. Then he went back to the kitchen for two of the big barrels in which the food refuse was kept, to be dumped overside for the fishes.

Sheltered by the hatch cover, Mustafa reis stripped naked and donned the thin twist of linen that was the dead man's only garment. He lowered the thin body into one of the barrels, then carried them both to the larboard rail.

The helmsman dozed at the wheel. In the maintop, the lookout was slumped in sleep. Mustafa reis smiled. He lifted the heavier barrel and emptied it, watching the body hit a following wave with a splash. He emptied the other barrel, then plodded back into the companionway.

In the kitchen he donned his own chainmail, trousers and slippers. He dropped the loincloth out the kitchen port. Then, picking up the breakfast tray, he moved from the kitchen along the narrow companionway to the door of the cabin where the Americano woman slept. He put the tray on the floor and scratched lightly at the door panels.

When he heard the bedropes creak, Mustafa whirled and fled for the safety of his own cabin, and a good sleep. When he was awakened Yussuf Caramanli would be dead and he Mustafa reis, fould be pasha of Tripoli in his place.

Eve Doremus stretched lazily in her little cabin bunk. She wore no clothing—there was no such thing as nightclothes in the Barbary states—and the red, early morning sun was a soothing warmth across her flesh. She was lazy with languid flesh and hazily remembered dreams. In those dreams, Stephen Fletcher had been pasha of Tripoli and she and Marlani his favorite wives, and whenever it was her turn to come to him on the seraglio divan, he always called Marlani. Until this very last time of all, just before the cook had scratched on her cabin door. She had gone angrily

93

into the selamlik, to find Fletcher calmly smoking a water-pipe and discussing types and manners of revenge with Mustafa reis. Fletcher, as pasha, had ordered the sea captain away, and had come to Eve, and—

She giggled, flushing, burrowing a little deeper into the cabin bunk. That had been a fine dream, but its memory was a pallid substitute for the real love her body needed. A little shocked, but secretly pleased at herself, Eve realized that the last night she had spent with Stephen Fletcher in his palace room was the most important night in all her life. It taught her she was, first and last, a woman. It was his hands that had brought her vividly to life and for the first time she had been warmed by a sense of fulfillment and emotional peace.

In the days and weeks since then, sailing across the Mediterranean in the *Burak*, she had been constantly near him. When he leaned against the rail, the wind whipping his yellow hair off his bronzed forehead, something pulled her to his side so that her hips could brush his, her shoulder press his own. More than once, she had wanted to whisper an invitation to him to tiptoe down to her little cabin when night closed in around the *Burak*. It wouldn't have been so brazen, for she had often read in his eyes the adoration the big American marine had for her.

"Land of mercy!" she whispered to the little cabin room. "If I don't stir myself and get his breakfast to him, Yussuf will have me whipped until Stephen won't want to look at me!"

She came off the bed and yawned, both white arms stretched toward the ceiling beams. Then she dove for the silken vest and thin, loose trousers in which she clad her body during the warm days on deck.

Just across the doorsill she found the platters of Balban figs and steaming porridge. With the tray in a hand she moved swiftly down the companionway and up onto the main deck. The ship was just stirring itself into wakefulness. Men were crouched in the rail shadows, munching sour black bread and dates. On the quarter-deck, Fletcher sat cross-legged before the deck tent, a curved scimitar before him.

Eve walked toward him, her eyes dancing, feeling his gaze ardently clinging to the smooth flowing curves of her body. Remembering her dreams, she smiled flirtatiously at him.

Then she was within the deck tent, sitting beside the divan on a hassock, placing the platter of food on the low, bedside table. The white kitten that was Marlani Chamiprak's plaything stretched and mewed, and rolled playfully over on its back.

"Run along, Piri," she whispered. But the kitten mewed and rubbed its back against her bare ankle.

Yussuf Caramanli sat up as Eve pressed thick cushions behind his back. His eyes were clear and bright, for he was nearly recovered. He even grumbled a little when Eve showed him the figs and porridge that Iskander had sent for his breakfast.

"Give me the figs and send the porridge back to the kitchen bins," he growled.

The kitten mewed plaintively, scratching lightly at Eve's foot with a soft paw.

"Little Piri would not scorn the barley paste," she told the pasha.

"Then give him some! I ought to make Iskander come up here and eat it off the floor the way the cat does!"

Eve bent and put a little of the mush on the deck planks. Piri sniffed at it and began to eat. He caught a clump of the wet barley with his teeth, chewing, dropping the little pellet and then retrieving it. Eve watched him for a moment.

"Highness, you must eat. Stefan says it is the only way in which you can recover your strength."

Yussuf Caramanli growled and grumbled, sliding lower into the cushions. "The figs will give me all the strength I need."

Eve held the silver bowl in her left hand, while her right selected a spoon. "You'd eat this if you could see the way little Piri is doing away with the—oh!"

She broke off and stared. There was such alarm in her voice that the pasha heaved himself onto an elbow to stare down at the little kitten. It was contorted into a ball of white fur, mewling piteously. It arched and jerked, writhing across the deck planks. A white froth come to its lips.

"Poison!" whispered Yussuf hoarsely.

His eyes bulged and he fell back, mouth open in horror. His hands went instinctively to his middle, almost feeling the pains that would have been convulsing him if he had eaten the gruel.

Eve sat frozen in shock. It occurred to her that she would

95

be suspected of poisoning the food, for it had been she who had tried to argue Yussuf into eating it. She stared at the kitten, not seeing Fletcher as he came running from the deck rail, not hearing Marlani Chamiprak cry out as she hurtled forward from the curtained section of the deck tent, where she had been completing her dressing.

Fletcher bent and picked up the kitten, it's body contorted in death. Marlani sobbed softly and came close to Fletcher, peering down at the animal. Then she turned and threw herself on her knees beside the pasha, weeping in a terrified frenzy.

Yussuf said, "The Americano girl is the guilty one! It was she who kept urging me to eat the porridge!"

Fletcher stepped forward. "I cannot believe that, pasha effendi. With you dead, Mustafa reis would take her, and me, and your *bash-kedin*. He would be pasha in your place. By killing you, she'd be dooming herself to death by torture. It doesn't make sense."

Yussuf Caramanli scowled thoughtfully. After a while he said, "No, it does not make sense. I know, as you know, that only my living body keeps Mustafa reis from his vengeance. But if it was not the Americano girl, who was it?"

Corsairs came running with bared blades, to scour the ship on the orders of a revitalized pasha. They returned with word that Iskander the cook could not be found. In his herb cabinet they had come across an empty glass vial that had held deadly poison.

"Iskander?" whispered Yussuf slowly. "Now why should my cook, who has been with me for twelve years, choose this time to put poison in my food?"

Yussuf Caramanli lay a while, silent, among his divan cushions. Then he smiled grimly and looked at Fletcher. "Mustafa reis is the man who did this. He's the only one on board ship with a sufficient motive, whose hate for you and the Americano girl, and his lust to become pasha in my place, would make him take such chances. Yet, I have no proof of this. Lacking proof, I cannot act, for Mustafa reis is a man strong among my people. You'll have to watch him, Stefan. Watch him to protect my life. That is my command."

As the days slid away to the gurgle of white sea foam

running under the keelboards, Yussuf pasha regained his strength swiftly. Now Fletcher was with him always, except while he oversaw the preparation of food. The freedom of the ship was his, and he moved among the corsairs with a lithe stride and arrogance in the swing of his wide' shoulders. These dark men gave way sullenly, and yet respectfully, for every man of them had seen his sabre-play when he held the quarter-deck stairs against the Spaniards.

Only Mustafa reis remained antagonistic, with a deadly calm that told Fletcher he was only waiting for another chance to rob the world of the man who held him back from vengeance. The sea captain would watch Fletcher with slitted eyes and a gentle smile on his lips, as though a fallen angel of Shaitan whispered words of promise into his ear.

Now Allah relented in his treatment of the *Burak*. At sunset on the second day after the white kitten had died, the corsair brig ran down a broad-beamed Greek schooner and boarded her almost without a fight. To the delight of every corsair, the schooner's hold bulged with gold ingots. With such a prize, the *Burak* needed only a safe harbor to make its journey fabulously successful. The sails remained aloft at night, and the helmsman steered by Polaris. A favoring wind came off the coast of Sicily to carry the *Burak* before it. Men could not sleep in the night, but remained awake, staring into the darkness, afraid that a distant glimmer was not the campfire of a fishing crew but the riding lights of a United States warship.

It was at the fifth hour of the night, when the sails creaked faintly overhead and the rush of water under the keel was louder than the whispers of the men hanging breathless at the railings, that Fletcher came toward the deck tent on silent, slippered feet. He had been below, to sleep a little against the night watch he would stand on the quarter-deck. He was a little early, for his sleep had been restless. The knowledge that the pasha of Tripoli had stumbled with the luck of sultan on a golden fortune weighted down his spirits.

The aga sat with Yussuf under the striped deck awning. His words carried easily in the stillness, and at the tone the man used, Fletcher paused and stood still.

"The gold is just one more proof of Allah's favor, blessed one! You've not forgotten the fleet you have been building at Zletin and Sabratha?"

"I have not forgotten, Ayub," said Yussuf Caramanli grimly. "More than fifty new ships, fitted out with the finest cannon my gold could buy in France and Spain. That's why this Greek ship is such a boon from Allah. It restores a fortune to my treasury rooms when they are most depleted."

The aga laughed softly. "Fifty brigs, each with twenty heavy guns, hidden now at Jerba. Enough to sweep the Americano fleet off the seas! And the best of it is, no one suspects. No, not even our own corsair captains!"

A low chuckle filled the air. "The less ears to hear, the less tongues to speak. I've been as secretive as a thief in the money pots. Now I only wait until the last of those fifty ships is complete with crew and gunpowder, and I'll take them out into the Mediterranean and teach the Americano dogs what it means to beard a Barbary pasha in his den!"

Fletcher felt his stomach heave. Anguish flooded in, paralyzing his legs and chest. A fleet of fifty brigs, each armed with twenty cannon! Even the *Constitution* and the *President* could not hope to stand against such sea power! If he himself had not known of such a weapon, hidden in the shoals near Jerba, Commodore Samuel Barron, who commanded the Mediterranean fleet in this blockade war against the Barbary state of Tripoli, could not possibly know.

He had heard no mention of a date when those ships would be properly outfitted and ready to be flung against the Americans, but he remembered the frantic activity that had taken the pasha to Zliten and Sabratha again and again while Marlani Chamiprak had strained her body to his in the deserted selamlik. Soon now, they would be ready.

He would have to move fast. Immediately upon their return to Tripoli, he would meet his friends in the Olive Tree Tavern and arrange for their escape. Eve Doremus would go with him; he would never leave her behind to face the fury of a betrayed Yussuf Caramanli!

CHAPTER 9

The Olive Tree Tavern was almost empty. The shadows cast by the hanging oil lamps were long and black, adding to the funereal pall that held the three men in its spell at the long wooden table. Wooden noggins of oily rum were moved in restless little circles across the table top.

"The damned double-dealer!"

It was Mark Avison who rasped the words, straightening suddenly, his pocked face flushed under unruly yellow hair. His wide shoulders flung back suddenly in anger, he lifted his big hand and banged his noggin of rum down hard so that the liquid spilled out and ran down his fingers.

"Easy, Mark. Easy," counselled the saturnine Framingham, his dark eyes bright. "We've nothing to go on but suspicions. True, Yuvaz hasn't sent us word as was promised, but—"

The man with the curly blond hair would not be mollified. He hunched forward on the wooden bench and thrust his scarred jaw forward. "What further proof do we need? He sent the little slave girl to find us—Shellah, her name is—and explain that he was working to get us horses and weapons. Now two weeks have gone by, and not a peep out of him! I don't like it. I wouldn't be surprised to learn he was betraying us to Yussuf, as soon as the pasha comes back from his little sea jaunt!"

"Hold your tongues!" hissed Ned Brunner.

The stocky Pennsylvanian was staring at the wide door of the tavern, his broad face an oaken mask. They could hear the footfalls themselves, now: one set of feet striding confidently, the other padding more softly, fearfully. Slowly, Brunner relaxed and his wide mouth quirked in a derisive smile.

"We're too highstrung, the lot of us. Fine ones, we are, to play at heroes escaping to freedom!"

Then his cold gray eyes widened, and his companions swiveled around on the bench. Stephen Fletcher was coming through the door out of the late spring night, one hand resting on the shoulder of Yuvaz the Armless.

Mark Avison stood up erect, and some of the anger in him spilled over. "It's good to see you, Steve, but that double-dealer with you—I wager a month's pay, if ever I collect pay as a marine again, that he's working with the pasha to betray us all!"

Fletcher chuckled and pushed Yuvaz onto the bench beside Ned Brunner. "Then you lose the bet. Yuvaz is with us, all the way. Right, Yuvaz?"

The armless man nodded silently, eagerly. His eyes were

feverishly bright as he hunched forward, writhing. If he had arms, he would have been hugging himself at the moment.

"It is true words Stefan speaks. A little while ago, I was undecided about betraying you. *Mashallah!* I admit it, you see. I was not concerned with whether a handful of Americanos escaped the walls of Tripoli so much as I was concerned over Hamet Caramanli, and his return to the throne!"

Mark Avison jerked forward, a big hand reaching out for the smaller Yuvaz. "So you'd have given us up to torture, would you, just to play your little game? And the desert girl, Shellah? What of her, eh? You'd have let her go to the rack, or be hung in a cage for the birds to eat?"

Fletcher moved against Avison, knocking him off balance to a sitting position on the bench. He was as big a man as the New Englander, and as strong. His hand held the former marine down and he said evenly, "Go easy, Mark! No harm's been done to Shellah, nor is any likely to come, as long as you keep your head. As long as we all keep our heads, for that matter. Yuvaz has been gathering swords and pistols, and horses and saddles, too, for us."

Caleb Framingham chuckled softly, his sombre eyes moving from Avison to Fletcher. His lank black hair hung uncut about his skinny neck, swirling a little as he bobbed his head at the armless man. "If he's done all that, Steve, why hasn't he sent us word? We've been worried sick."

Fletcher smiled grimly. "He's been busy in other ways. Tell them, Yuvaz!"

The armless man writhed ecstatically, his black eyes rolling in his head. "I've had word from the Tauregs, in from the oasis of Jaghbub! They brought news that Hamet Caramanli has joined forces with the Americanos!"

"God's my life!" exclaimed the suspicious Brunner, wide mouth opening. "I don't believe it!"

Framingham waved a bony hand for silence. "Go on, go on!"

Yuvaz said eagerly, "You remember William Eaton, the Americano who was United States consul at Tunis, back in 1799?"

Fletcher added, "He's been made a general since then. My father told me once he served under Washington during our Revolution."

100

Yuvaz nodded. "He is the man. At the outbreak of Yussuf's war with your country, Eaton was still your consul at Tunis. When the *Philadelphia* went down, he decided that the only way the war could be brought to a successful finish was to depose Yussuf and put Hamet back on the throne as pasha. I did not know this until very recently, when I talked to the Jaghbub nomads."

The armless man spoke on, and it was Avison who brought a noggin of rum to him and held it so he could drink. Eagerly, Yuvaz resumed his tale. He spoke of the fact that Eaton and Consul General James L. Cathcart of Tripoli— who left that city at the outset of the war— decided they would undertake an expeditionary attack on Tripoli by land, to act in conjunction with the sea blockade under Commodore Edward Preble, then commanding the fleet. To receive support for this venture, Eaton returned to the United States in the spring of 1803, where he appeared before President Thomas Jefferson and the Congress of the United States of America.

Eaton was appointed navy agent, and directed to act with Commodore Samuel Barron, who was replacing Preble as commander of the Mediterranean squadron. In midsummer, 1804, Commodore Barron took the *U. S. S. President* to Tripoli with General William Eaton as a passenger. Put ashore at Alexandria, Egypt, Eaton began communicating with Hamet Caramanli, to secure his cooperation in a land assault on Tripoli.

All these matters took time, and much secrecy. Hamet was naturally suspicious, Yuvaz stated apologetically, for if their attack should fail, death would be his gift from Yussuf. Lieutenant P. J. O'Bannon of the United States Marine Corps and Midshipman George Mann of the *Argus* were his American companions as he conducted his negotiations with the ex-pasha of Tripoli. It was agreed that Hamet would rouse up the local sheiks, and bring a force of Barbary Arabs to fight together with the United States marines and Greek mercenaries under Eaton and O'Bannon. A caravan of baggage camels would carry their equipment.

Their march began in March, 1805, from Marabout.

They traveled by way of sand valleys and rocky lowlands, fighting the greed of local sheiks and the mercurial enthusiasms and depairs of the Tripolines who rode with Hamet Caramanli. They made from five to twenty miles a day,

101

across a hot, barren land where the thermometer registered over one hundred and fifty degrees day after day. There were revolts to be overcome, and lagging spirits to be cheered or lashed into barbaric eagerness. Slowly but steadily, the little expedition moved westward across the coastal shore of northern Africa.

April found the Bedouin sheiks deserting in large numbers. They were at Sidi Barrani when Eaton faced the treacherous sheik, El Taiib, and threatened to shoot him down as an enemy if he gave more trouble. This breach of relations was patched up, and the march went on, but the Qued Ali tribesmen were fickle and insincere in their friendliness, though their large herds of goats and sheep, camels, horses and cattle had added meat to the rice diets of the Americans.

Yuvaz shook his head and looked sorrowful. "I could not understand this attitude of the desert peoples. Hamet was their pasha. They should have welcomed the chance to put him back on his throne!"

Brunner grinned sardonically. "They don't have your faith. Maybe they heard about your arms."

Yuvaz scowled for a moment, then showed his white teeth in a mirthless grin. "Yussuf will lose more than his arms if Hamet becomes pasha. I, myself, will personally direct his torture!"

Avison shivered, staring into the maniacal eyes. He gestured abruptly, and growled, "How close to Tripoli are they now?"

From Sollum to Bardia and beyond, there were more threats of revolt, explained Yuvaz. Once the American marines faced their desert allies with rifles at the ready when a disaffection threatened the food supply. The lack of water, Yuvaz admitted, more than once contributed to revolt. At an old Roman ruin, they were obliged to drink water with two dead men floating in it. To top this, the *Argus* was late at the rendezvous point off Bomba.

On the morning of April 16, the *Argus* hove into sight, followed two days later by the *Hornet*. Equipped with good food and fresh water, the expedition pressed on toward Derna. Eaton had brought a mutinous band of desert sheiks, fickle officers and janissaries of a deposed pasha, and a handful of American sailors and marines six hundred miles across a sweltering land where heat and sand and lack of water were enough to drive men mad. But now his cannon pointed down at Derna, and Derna commanded the land gates of the city of Tripoli.

Yuvaz laughed harshly and stared around him at the intent Americans.

"At one time, I could not make up my mind whether to betray you and earn the good graces of Yussuf so that I might continue to plot against him, or help you to spite him. All that is forgotten, now. The Americanos are allies of my lord, Hamet the Blessed. So you are my allies. I have scimitars and pistols, bags of gunpowder and shot, hidden in the cellars of my friends. There are fleet horses, too, with saddles for their backs, ready to carry you to safety. You will ride the coastal road to Derna, where your General Eaton is in command."

"He took the place, then?" asked Framingham.

Yuvaz nodded. "After a fight of two and a half hours. Eighty-five men he had—against ten times that number!" The armless man shrugged. "There were two thousand Arabs under Hamet, but—" Yuvaz spat in disgust—"they were hired with money given Hamet the Blessed by your General Eaton. It was not the Bedawi tribesmen who won Derna, but the American marines and the Greek cannoneers who fought with them!

"That is why you can now escape from Tripoli by land. You have Derna to escape to. You men will be welcomed by Hamet, for you know the defenses of Tripoli better than any except Yussuf's own captains. I myself will go with you, as guide and interpreter."

Yuvaz fell silent, to drink again as Avison held the noggin to his mouth. He sat silent, now, listening to the excited voices of the Americans swirl around him. The years were bringing his vengeance near, and Yuvaz hugged the moment with every wild beat of his fanatical heart.

Fletcher was saying, "We'll leave tomorrow night. We've got to get word to Commodore Barron about that secret fleet! He's going to have to smash that now, if he can, before it's ready to go to sea against him."

"There'll be the *Argus* or the *Hornet* at Derna, ready to carry word. How soon can we be there, Caleb?"

The lank New Yorker scowled thoughtfully. "Derna's roughly seven hundred miles from Tripoli. A fast horseman can make that distance in a little less than ten days. If we leave the Cyrenaica Gate at midnight, we'll be there in plenty of time."

"If Yussuf doesn't catch us and bring us back," growled Brunner gloomily.

Yuvaz shook his head, "Yussuf Caramanli will not know for sure whether the American forces will be marching west along the desert roads of Cyrenaica toward Tripoli. He will not dare leave the city to chase a few escaped slaves! He'll prefer to remain here, where he is strongest!"

Fletcher nodded. "And where he can keep a finger on his hidden fleet, to hurl it out against the blockading ships when it's ready." He drew a deep breath, then added grimly. "Let's hope he doesn't do that until we've gotten word to Barron!"

The girl was waiting in the shadow of a marble trellis as Fletcher came striding through the palace gardens, past the flower squares and the dolphin fountain that splashed its crystal waters into the wide pool below. She came forward with a faint clash of bangles and necklaces, her soft dark eyes glowing brightly under the gold-threaded rim of her hood.

"Stefan, I came to warn you—"

"Shellah!"

"Hssst! No noise! Marlani has sent Eve to the haremlik, to stitch seed pearls onto some divan cushions. Instead of Eve, you'll find Marlani waiting in your room."

Fletcher drew a deep breath, feeling anger and panic rising in him. That amorous she-cat! If she got in his way, he'd wring her soft brown throat with his own hands! The lives of a score or more Americans, including that of Eve Doremus herself, depended on a swift escape tomorrow night! Should Yussuf pasha catch his favorite wife and himself together in his little room, there'd be no escape except to the torture dungeons.

"The fool! That stupid little mink of a fool girl!"

Shellah smiled, but there was anxiety in her eyes. "You won't let her change your plans, Stefan?"

Her worry caught his ear. He remembered something that Mark Avison had said, earlier this night. Fletcher grinned. "He's a big brute, isn't he?"

Shellah flushed and let her eyes fall. "Mark Avison promised he'd come back for me when the Americanos put Yussuf off the throne."

"And they will, if Marlani doesn't upset our little apple-cart with her heat!"

Shellah whispered a prayer to Allah as Fletcher whirled on a heel and moved across the garden path toward the arched portico of the selamlik quarters, where the grillwork windows glimmered like fairy tracings in the moonlight. His mind balanced Marlani Chamiprak and her appetites against everything he planned, and he was alarmed at the small, mocking voice of doubt in him. He knew well enough what the *bash-kedin* wanted, and the dangers in giving in to her, but he didn't know what his reaction to her would be.

He found himself rationalizing that he could take her as she asked, and run the risk of being found by Yussuf Cara-manli. Or he could attempt to dissuade her, plead the dangers of discovery, and hope that for once, she would let reason rule her flesh. As his fingers stretched for the doorpull, Stephen Fletcher told himself that whatever happened, it was the will of fate. I'm becoming as fatalistic as a Turk, he thought, and opened the heavy wooden door.

Marlani Chamiprak lay on the little bed propped up against fat, tasseled cushions. Her black hair was gathered high on her head, in thick coils fixed with golden pins. A transparent black *khalak* was wrapped about her lithe body.

"Close the door, Stefan," she whispered.

"Are you mad, to come here like this? Always before, it was in the selamlik, when Yussuf was away at Sabratha or Zliten!"

She stretched lazily, and golden bangles clashed musically as they slipped from her wrists to her elbows. For an hour she had waited here, letting the explosive hunger of her appetite build slowly, knowing that shortly this big blond Americano would be in her arms and that powerful body be once again at her command. The fact that Yussuf was within these same palace walls only added to the flavor of this meeting.

"Close the door, Stefan," she whispered again.

Her eyes glittered under their long black lashes. Her full mouth, wet and red, lay like a tempting, overripe fruit in the dusky copper of her face. Fletcher admitted, even as he heard the door latch click behind him, that she was a living torment to the senses. He loved Eve Doremus, and he would

105

have died for her, but this girl from the sand country of inner Libya was a succubus!

"Now come here, and sit beside me."

Her hand patted the edge of the low rope-bed. As he lowered himself to the mattress, Fletcher said hoarsely, "You're playing with fire, Marlani. If Yussuf suspected we were here—"

"He almost caught us after that fight with the Spaniard, didn't he? I wonder what he thought when he saw me kissing you? Did he really believe what we told him later, that it was out of gratitude?" She laughed softly, and slid lower against the cushions, so that a fold of the thin black veil slipped, and a naked shoulder glowed softly in the lamplight. "And if he believes that lie, will he also wonder what else I might do—in gratitude?"

Her hand touched his wrist and ran up the arm to the hard shoulder, her palm like smooth, fiery satin. The silvered nails dug into his flesh, stinging him. Against the black silk of the *khalak* her pointed breasts began to rise and fall swiftly.

"Danger stimulates me, Stefan," she moaned. "To think that Yussuf might walk in that door at any moment—"

She rose suddenly to fling herself against him, head bent a little sideways as her mouth found his, strong young arms around him, straining her body to him.

Marlani never thought of her heritage from savage forebears, from men who lived out their lonely, nomad lives between the oases of Kufra and of Jaghbub, from women raised only that they might study means and ways to bring men pleasure. She only knew that in her flesh lived an insatiable desire for the frenzy of love, a primeval need to perform it in danger, to hurt and be hurt, in inseparable ecstasies of pleasure and pain. As her fingernails scraped along his back, rousing an animal cry from his lungs, she laughed and twisted away.

He lunged after her. One hand caught a fold of her thin black veil and tugged. Then Marlani was whirling on bare feet, her golden anklets tinkling, and the *khalak* was pulling free, baring her body.

For an instant she paused, quiet, arms held high—then she flung herself against him.

At that same instant the door opened.

Yussuf Caramanli stood there, legs spread, eyes like bright black coals.

Marlani Chamiprak screamed. She clawed at Fletcher's chest with her painted nails and the body that had strained toward him now arched furiously away from him.

"Yussuf! Yussuf! Protect you *bash-kedin!* The Americano is like a mad dog!"

"You foul bitch," the pasha whispered. "Like an alley cat, slinking here and there for your pleasures!"

He came forward. As Marlani shrank from him, the back of his hand caught her alongside the jaw and drove her stumbling back against the wall. The veins in his temples throbbed with rage, and his jaw muscles worked convulsively.

"Should I bury you to your neck in the sand, you desert whore? Or flay you alive, and hang you up on hooks above the slave market?"

The woman whimpered and went to her knees. Her face fell forward into her hands, and the thick black hair came flooding down across her wrists and forearms to veil her body. Almost soundlessly, she sobbed in great jerking heaves.

Yussuf Caramanli looked at Fletcher.

The American had never seen hatred like this. It rose from within and distorted the man, mottling his flesh, reddening his bulging eyes and twisting the hard lips into a horrible grimace. And yet it seemed that the pasha was trying to control that rage, to think calmly while every nerve and muscle in his body urged a hot, quick revenge.

"As for you, you nasrany boar, I'll make you wish you'd never been born before I'm through! Molten lead poured down your throat will be too quick—the flayer's knife too easy! I need time—time in which to outdo Mustafa reis in your punishment!"

Yussuf gestured and several of his palace guards, who had been standing at the doorway waiting, came forward and grasped Fletcher's arms, bending them up behind his back. Grimly, Fletcher succumbed. To get away now, he would have to overcome a whole city. Worse than the thought of his own approaching tortures was his betrayal of the Americans of the Oliver Tree Tavern. Mark Avison, Caleb Framingham, Ned Brunner: they would wait in vain, now, for their escape. And the *U. S. S. Constitution,* and the *Argus,* patrol-

107

ling the Mediterranean, would be blown out of those waters by the hidden fleet that Yussuf pasha was hiding along the shoals of the African coastline.

The guardsmen forced him from the room, bent forward before them as their hands twisted his wrists up against his shoulder blades. Behind him, he could hear Marlani Chamiprak scream in utter terror.

CHAPTER 10

An ominous silence lay over the Caramanli palace. From the entrance passageway to the smallest vase-niche in the haremlik, no man spoke above a whisper. Bare feet padded about on necessary duties, and guards stood frozen at their posts before doors and gateways, hands on their long scimitars. But outside of this, there seemed no life at all behind the thick white walls. Yussuf pasha was in the selamlik, mad with rage, ordering whippings and the bastinado to any who went near him. The *bash-kedin* sobbed in helpless terror on the cushions of her seraglio divan.

In one of the damp, small rooms of the dungeons that lay beneath the castello, Stephen Fletcher was stretched on his back, hands behind his head. Three hours before, he had been thrust through the great iron door that was the entryway to these cold, wet cellars, and the iron bolts slammed home behind him. Then he had been brought along a narrow corridor between empty, dark vaults fitted with iron bars or solid iron gates, and hurled savagely into a tiny square of stone and metal whose only furniture was a long, wide bench of rotting wood that served as bed and table, chair and couch.

He was felt dead inside, filled with a heavy despair that weighed him down as grimly as any manacles. Disgust ate in him, too: disgust at his own susceptibility to a little exposed flesh. Hindsight told him that he should have lifted Marlani Chamiprak and put her outside his door and locked it. He had known the pasha was suspicious of them, yet he had let the woman kiss and stir him until reason flew away before the fever of desire.

His fist hit the edge of the wide bench.

"Fool, fool, fool! With everything to gain by prudence, I was like a sailor after a half-year voyage!"

108

He reviled himself, trying not to think of the tortures that Yussuf Caramanli would be dreaming up in his selamlik. It would not be an easy death. There would be no merciful quickness, no volley of shots or headsman's falling axe. Stephen Fletcher would suffer, and for a long time.

The palace was so quiet above him that he wondered if he was losing his hearing. When the faint pad of feet on stone sounded from the dark corridor, he swung himself from the bench and came to a stand, heart pounding madly. So soon? Was Yussuf so eager to begin his cruel play that he would begin now, in the middle of the night? Surely he would wait for dawn, if only to give Fletcher more strength to survive prolonged torture.

But these weren't the footfalls of armed guards, there was no arc of light from a gaoler's lantern, no jingle of keys —only bare feet padding, then the sibilant sound of short, quick breathing.

Fletcher walked catlike to the barred door and stared out into the gloom. A woman was standing there, in loose silk trousers and vest, looking fearfully behind her.

"Shellah," he whispered, and the woman jumped.

She came closer, and Fletcher could see the big iron key in her hand.

"Yuvaz got the key," she panted, clinging to the cell bars. "He's stolen dozens of them in the years he's been here, waiting for the moment to strike at Yussuf. He says we have to free you, so you can get word to the Americans about the secret fleet."

She bent, thrusting her key in the lock, praying that no click of falling tumbler would betray her presence to the guard in the outer corridor. The lock turned smoothly, the door opened silently and Fletcher was in the corridor beside her, taking the key from her trembling hand.

He closed and locked the cell door, noting that in the gloom of the corridor no casual eye would notice whether there was anyone inside or not.

"Eve? What of Eve?"

"She's safe enough in the haremlik. I left her crying her pretty eyes out for you."

"I was an idiot!"

Shellah smiled wisely. "Say instead that Marlani is a determined cat, who likes her loving heavily spiced with peril."

Her soft, fragrant fingers over his lips held him silent for a moment, and he could read the warning in her eyes. There were guards patrolling these corridors. Mostly they slept or played chess in one of the anterooms. But there were times when Yussuf Caramanli took it into his head to come visiting a prisoner; and then it would not be good to be caught with an ivory chesspiece in hand, or slumped sideways in dreams about the slave girl one was saving up his zequins to buy. This night was a time to be alert.

"Do not speak until I tell you, Stefan," she whispered. "Just follow me!"

He crept after her like her shadow. They slipped through an unoccupied cell by way of a loose stone slab and soon found themselves in another part of the cellar entirely, amid cells equipped with manacles that had imprisoned Greeks and Carthaginians in the days of the Scipios. Now Shellah went more surely, for there were no guards in this old, closed section of the castello.

A little side door with a carefully broken bolt opened onto a paved walk winding under a rose arbor and coming to a stop before a low wooden door in the garden gate. There were no guards here: the prisoners were inside the palace walls, so what chance had they of reaching the gardens? A latch clicked, then Shellah was draping the hem of her garment across her face so that only her dark eyes and brows could be seen.

Side by side, they hurried along the cobbled street, under the lighted eyes of windows in the stucco walls. Then the moonlight was flooding the shore, the clumps of esparto grass throwing black shadows across the white sands. Their sandaled feet kicked up little puffs of sand as they moved along, almost in the shadow of the high, thick sea walls, toward a narrow jut of beach that ran outward at low tide like an elongated finger into the sea. An overturned catboat lay by the tiny promontory.

"A fisherman brought it here at dusk," whispered Shellah, bending to help Fletcher turn it over. "There is food in oilskin wrappings in the gear locker, and fishing tackle, and a woolen barracan against the cold."

"You've thought of everything."

She looked at Fletcher and now he could see the tears glinting crystal in her eyes. Fletcher remembered Mark Avison and his solicitude for this desert girl.

"I wish it were you and Mark getting into this," he said.

110

Her smile was tremulous. "Yuvaz says you have the better chance to make it. He could not get in touch with Mark Avison at the Olive Tree Tavern. Besides, he is not certain that Mark trusts him fully. And by freeing you, Yuvaz is able to strike at Yussuf. The pasha will be mad with rage when he learns you have escaped."

"And you? Will any harm come to you?"

Shellah shrugged. "Most likely not. Who would accuse me of risking my neck to save a nasrany?"

Something about her hesitant speech made Fletcher scan her face more closely. He guessed her thoughts. "You think Eve will suffer? Is that it?"

"He'll probably put her in a dungeon, in a fit of temper. But she's well guarded tonight. He'll know she could not have helped you get away. Yussuf will be angry, but he'll be cunning. I don't think he'll hurt her—not until he recaptures you, at any rate."

Fletcher groaned. If there were any chance at all to stay and fight, to win freedom with the woman he loved, he would have kicked the boat away from him. His head ached from the pound of blood in his veins and the constriction that gripped his heart. Eve, Eve! he thought. I'll come back for you. On my life, I promise it! Then he was bending and putting strong hands to the small boat. Wood scraped on sand as the narrow keel slid forward into the water.

Fletcher turned to the girl. "Will you be safe on the way back?"

She laughed softly. "If a guard sees me, I'll tell him I was visiting a friend on the beach, to make love a little. On a warm night like this, there'll be a hundred men and women in the dunes, trying to forget the boredom of their lives."

The American nodded and said goodby. He swung into the skiff and it went sliding out into the harbor waters. A mast was tilted upward from the stern, tied across the forward thwart. A triangular sail and rigging lay neatly wrapped on the floorslats.

It took a few moments to unwrap the ropes and seat the mast. He ran up the sail and the wind shook it, then filled it slowly, until the canvas strained and the boom swung outward to the full length of its mainsheet. The skiff was cat-rigged, without shrouds or bowsprit, but it took the water easily and there was speed in its lean hull. Fletcher felt a small glow of animal pleasure as the wind whipped him and

111

the boat surged forward like a living thing. He was remembering for an instant the years of his youth, when he had sailed catboats in Accokeek Creek, and the smell of the salt tides and marshes and the clear, high calling of the gulls. Then, there had been high adventure in every clump of marshgrass. Now there was death behind and death ahead, and the sense of adventure was gone in the grim necessity of staying alive.

Moonlight tipped the little wavecrests with white fire as the skiff slid past the black, wet rocks of the mole. Fletcher squatted on the aft thwart, gripping the long wooden handle of the tiller and telling himself what a miracle it was that he was here, a free man, while less than an hour ago he had been sunk in bitter gloom in the castello dungeon.

And yet, when he considered it, it didn't seem so strange. The pashas and beys of this Barbary Coast were served by men with the fatalism of the East in their hearts. Most Arabs or Turks would never think in terms of escape from a palace prison. They accepted death and punishment as they accepted everything else: with a belief in foreordained design that would be comic, were it not so tragic. There was little need for wide-awake guards when the prisoners viewed their imprisonment as the will of Allah.

If he and Shellah had been seen leaving the castello gardens, they had been looked on as lovers slipping to a bed on the warm Mediterranean sands. Now all that remained was to elude a possible onlooker from the anchored boats in the roadstead. Fletcher knew that the hour was an early one, but he could pass for an ambitious fisherman, anxious to lower his nets before the dawn.

No challenging voice came across the waters. No yellow lantern was lifted high to illuminate the little cockboat. It slipped between the rocks and through the shallow waters until the jutting mole was behind it, and only the vast stretch of heaving Mediterranean before it.

The silence of the sea was all around him as the shoreline and its flickering lights faded astern. The restless waves lifted and carried the tiny skiff forward like a leaf, as the wind in the sails and his hand on the tiller kept her prow pointing north. She ran before the wind and following sea with her sail fat and her freeboards slicing water.

All that night Fletcher sailed, until dawn was a red haze in the east and the seas seemed turned to blood. Now hunger ate in him and he blessed Yuvaz and Shellah with every mouthful of the meat and bread he chewed.

The sun came up and made a pleasant heat on his back and shoulders. Soon he took off his shirt and sat naked to the middle, his feet bare. He had no way of knowing how long he sailed, but after a time he trimmed in the mainsheet and let the boom swing over as he jibed, and now he sailed with the wind abeam, eastward toward Derna.

Somewhere out on these lifting. blue waters, he should sight an American warship. If that fortune failed him, he would find William Eaton in his captured citadel along the Cyrenaica sands.

Night came swirling in with a thick, wet fog that blotted out the sky and everything about him but the heaving sea. Without a compass he was afraid he would lose his way. He made a crude sea anchor and tossed it overside. Then he wrapped himself in the thick woolen barracan and stretched out on the floor slats. As his heavy eyelids closed wearily, he remembered that he had not slept now for more than twenty hours.

The fog lasted all the next day, hanging low to the water and coming in thick white puffs where the wind caught it. Fletcher cursed the fog and the lack of a compass that held him here, immobile. He dared not move without knowing his direction, for the entire coastline was a network of Tripoline spies and allies, and in the fog he could not tell east from west or north from south.

During his second night at anchor the fog lifted. Fletcher woke to the sun on his face and a fair wind coming down from Italy. Just in time, too, he thought, wolfing the last crust of bread tinted yellow by sulphur. The water cask was more than half full, but his food was gone. He stood and stretched, then bent to unreef the sail where he had tied it along the boom.

He paused like that, his fingers on the gaskets.

A sail was just visible, a tiny white triangle where greenish water met blue sky. Fletcher needed no second look to know it was no American sail. A ship like the *Constitution* or the *Constellation* would be higher in the sky with its towering topgallants. This was a Barbary brig or felucca heading toward him.

He worked swiftly, hoping that he had not been seen. He unseated his mast and placed it in the bottom of the boat,

113

sails beside it. Then he stretched himself out on the keel-boards and waited. He had made his hull as low as possible and there was nothing else he could do. With only his eyes and the top of his head showing above the gunwale-capping, he waited.

The ship did not veer, but ran straight on with the wind abeam. Within half an hour, Fletcher knew her lookout had sighted him.

He chuckled bitterly, and came to his feet. "I could up sail and try to run, but she'd catch me in less than an hour. As well wait and take what she has to give."

But Fletcher was not a man who could sit and wait for his doom. He whirled and dove for the mast, cursing between his teeth. His heart thudding wildly, he set it up and ran up the sail and watched the wind fill it. As his left hand took the tiller, his right fist came down hard on the gunwale-capping.

"She's got to travel fast to catch you, Stephen Fletcher!" he shouted. "Maybe it won't be as easy as you thought!"

The skiff was small and fast, and Fletcher fled with the wind running. As the strange ship came on, he put the tiller to windward at right angles to his former course. It took the felucca longer to come about, and he gained a few precious cable lengths.

He ran for half the day, until the superior speed of the corsair ship brought it within shooting distance. From the shrouds, three musketeers hung with their legs in the shrouds and peppered shot at him.

Sooner or later one of those balls would cripple him. With a sigh, Fletcher put his rudder hard down and watched the sails slat above him. He sat unmoving as the boat checked its headway and swung lazily upward in the heave of a wave.

"I'm cursed," he said, and bitterness filled his throat.

Half naked men swirled overside from the felucca into a long tender. and came for him, rowing smoothly. An aga stood in the prow, a cocked pistol in either hand, the wind stretching his topknot out behind him.

"Come aboard, nasrany dog!" he shouted.

As the cockboat scraped against the skiff, Fletcher vaulted into the smaller boat. Black eyes stared ferociously, and one or two of the men grinned, running their eyes over his big body. The aga laughed cruelly.

"They're wondering how long you'll take the torture Yussuf has dreamed up," he informed him. "Or perhaps how well you'll take the kiss of the cat on board the *Aydah*."

"The cat?"

"Our captain must have some pleasure from the chase, nasrany."

A cold chill started up Fletcher's spine. As the mocking eyes of the aga moved past him toward the corsair ship, the American swung around. A man leaned against the starboard rail, grinning down at him. Fletcher would know that sardonic brown face anywhere.

Mustafa reis!

The corsair captain's bright eyes never moved from the American as he scaled the rope ladder, vaulted onto the deckboards and came to stand before him. The wind aft stirred the folds of Mustafa's barracan, and sent his loose, baggy trousers rippling about his legs. His fingers worked spasmodically on the braided haft of his curved dagger.

"Your luck has turned, nasrany," he said at last, and the passion in him slurred his voice. "Allah has rewarded me at last for the many gifts I've put in his mosques. Now you're in my hands."

Fletcher shrugged. He had done what he could to run from these pirates, but it was not enough. No words would change whatever fate Mustafa reis prepared for him.

The corsair captain smiled almost affably. "Shortly now, you'll be back at the castello of the Caramanlis. There are people eager to see you there—Yussuf pasha, his unfaithful wife, Marlani, who claims you were raping her when Yussuf interrupted, Eve Doremus—"

Fletcher started forward, then felt the cold round muzzle of a pistol shoved into the small of his back. Mustafa reis laughed in delight.

"That stirs you, eh, nasrany? Let me tell you this, then: Yussuf has thrown your precious Christian woman into a dungeon cell! Down into the dampness with the castello rats! He'll keep her there a month; if you aren't back in his power by that time, he'll torture her to death in the great square! That is, if I can't talk him into giving her to me. I'd like to enjoy her charms for a while, before I give her to my slaves . . ."

The pistol was not enough to hold him now. Like a cat he moved, knowing that a pistol ball would be a blessing compared to what waited for him in Tripoli. His hands went out and his long, powerful fingers closed around the throat of Mustafa reis. Unbalanced by the attack, the corsair captain rode back on his heels and fell to the deck.

Twisting and turning, they rolled from the scuppers to the main hatch. Voices were yelling all around them, but Fletcher didn't hear. His only concern was choking the life from this devil before him. It didn't matter what they did to him, if only Mustafa reis died here and now.

His fingers dug deeper. The bright eyes below him bulged. Mustafa reis heaved up, but Fletcher was too big and too strong for him to dislodge. They rolled against the naked legs that hemmed them in.

Around them, men cursed and swore by Allah and his prophet. Mustafa reis had given orders that this man was not to be killed under any circumstances. Yussuf pasha had promised to torture him to death in the great market square, over a period of thirty days. It would be a fine sight to see a nasrany take thirty days to die, with each hour of those days an eternity of pain and screaming suffering! And the man or men who killed him would take his place: this was Mustafa reis' own solemn promise.

But by the beard of Allah! If they did not free their captain's throat from those fingers, he would die!

One man braver than the rest shifted his grip on the curved handle of his long-barreled pistol. He brought it up and sideways, so that the barrel slammed against Fletcher's temple.

The big Americano did not go down. The pistol lifted and fell again. The man who used it tempered his blows, for fear of killing the mad Americano. Five times Fletcher was hit before he stiffened and rolled free of the choking, sobbing Mustafa reis, to lie face upward on the deck planks.

Mustafa reis was bent double, a hand to his red and swollen throat, sucking air painfully into his lungs. Eager hands reached out to him, lifting him to his feet. His face was black with congested blood, and twisted with hatred.

"Lash his wrists to the shrouds!"

The corsair lifted himself erect, trying to fight the nausea that thickened his throat. He watched the half naked Fletcher lifted and dragged toward the starboard shrouds. Men scrambled into the netting, wrapping bits of hemp about the American's wrists and heaving upward until he

116

was stretched in the shrouds like a man crucified.

Mustafa reis whispered hoarsely, "Leave him like that, for the rest of the day and all night long. Tomorrow, a little after dawn, we'll flog him!"

CHAPTER 11

The night was an endless thing to the man who hung spread-eagled on the shrouds. An offshore wind had come out of the Sahara, its fading warmth touching him at chest and face in an effervescent searching. The sea lifted and dipped below him, the ropes sawing at his tied wrists and ankles at each movement of the brig. After a while the pain at his wrists was so intense it seemed the rope was slicing through them, and blood ran down his arms in rivulets. Dawn found him only half conscious, his head lolling limply.

When Mustafa reis saw him like that, he roared in anger.

"Cut his thongs, you sons of Shaitan! Am I to whip a dead man? I want to hear him scream!"

Steel flashed in the growing sunlight, and hands cradled Fletcher to the deck planks. Wine from a leather jack was poured down his throat, and brown hands fed him spiced meats and hot bread. When the strength began to flow back into him, he could see that his wrists had been cleaned and bandaged.

Mustafa reis stood before him, legs spread wide, white teeth bared in a wolfish grin. "Allah would have me keep you sound of limb, nasrany, until Yussuf gives you to his torturers. Besides, if I let you grow too weak, you'll be no fun under the cat." The black eyes searched him carefully, seeing that the food and drink was putting new life into the American. Then Mustafa laughed harshly and gestured with a hand. "Tie him to the mainmast."

Four men lifted Fletcher to the thick cedar mast. His arms were tied around the mainmast in grotesque embrace, his cheek tight against the wood. He felt the shirt torn from his back, and his tanned skin bared to the sea breeze. From somewhere behind him, he heard Mustafa reis say, "Begin!"

Leather swished in the air, and his back exploded with pain.

The plaits of leather, sewn with tiny pellets of lead, were like tongues of fire biting through his skin. Fletcher hit the mast with his whole body, convulsing, his mouth opening in an involuntary groan.

The thongs came down again, but Fletcher stood rigid, soundless, though his muscles cramped in protest. Then a violent shudder ran the length of his body, shaking the stout mast that held him.

Again the leaden pellets drove into him, exposing rib bones and red flesh.

Fletcher threw back his head, wanting to scream as he had wanted nothing before in all his life. Silently, he ground his teeth into his lip, until there was warm blood in his mouth, and swung his head from side to side.

Then he saw the ship: a big frigate, with an immense spread of snowy sail and brass cannon gleaming brightly in the sun. A curving gilded beak rose above the sharp prow that came slicing through the green waves. She was fast and graceful, this American frigate, and her forty-four guns showed her power. Only seven years old—she had slid off her chocks at Hartt's shipyard in Boston in the fall of '98— the *Constitution* was already building a reputation. She was hull up and coming fast, sails tight and full with wind.

Fletcher did not believe his eyes. Through tight-clamped teeth he groaned, "I'm going mad with the pain. I'm beginning to see visions!"

A puff of white smoke appeared at one of the frigate's forward cannon. An instant later his ears caught the dull thud.

The whiplash about to strip his back of more flesh paused in mid-stroke. A man cried out harshly from the port rail. Then other voices broke in, and feet went running back and forth on the deck. Mustafa reis was bellowing orders. Powder kegs were broken out, and men came to carry them to their battle stations.

Fletcher hung on the mast, forgotten. His eyes were wide, his twisted grin triumphant. "Hell! It's the *Constitution* herself! I'd know her lines anywhere! Cave in her timbers, you American swabs! Fill her full of holes, then ride your keel over her settling hull!"

His voice rose to a screech. "Mustafa reis, you damned pirate! You hear me? Take a good look at her. She's the *Constitution* herself that's found you! You can't outrun her and you can't outfight her! Maybe now you'll learn what it means to start a war with the United States!"

118

He was shouting and laughing and crying all at the same time. A passing corsair heard him babbling and backhanded him as he went by, but Fletcher only laughed the louder. Now the *Constitution* was swinging broadside on and her starboard cannon were like little round mouths pointing at the Tripoline. For a few moments she rode like this, beautiful and tall and sleek, her white sails bulging, slicing easily through the Mediterranean. Then the cannon mouths were spitting red flame and white smoke, and as the roar of those brass voices came to Fletcher, the deck rocked under him. It was as if a giant hand caught the brig and shook her. A mast came down and hit the deck with a screech of splitting wood. Sheered-off ropes whipped in the wind. Men were screaming belowdecks, helpless in that hailstorm of crushing lead.

Almost leisurely, the *U. S. S. Constitution* veered off. She ran with the wind ahead of the Barbary ship, and swung about five hundred yards away. As she returned, almost impudent in her swift strength, her port cannon menaced the pirate vessel.

Mustafa reis screamed with rage on the quarter-deck. "Starboard helm! Starboard helm! Clear the decks below!"

Men ran to obey those commands, but the American frigate was coming fast. When she was directly to larboard, her cannon—twenty-two to each side—belched their lead and flame and smoke again.

The *Aydah* shuddered wildly, trembling like a living thing in agony under that smashing broadside. Wood splintered; timbers caved. Powderkegs went up in red geysers. A sail flapped uselessly where the mizzenmast had been shot away. The quarter-deck guns were firing high as the gun-deck cannon were firing low, drowning out the screams of Mustafa reis from the starboard rail.

Fletcher was laughing, helplessly, inanely.

"Again, again, again!" he howled. "Fill her up with lead and let the damned ship go down to Davy Jones's locker! Come up on her starboard planks this time!"

The corsair brig was listing badly, exposing her belly timbers. Her starboard cannon were pointing skyward as the ship tilted. She could not have harmed the big American frigate from any angle, now. As if realizing that, the *Constitution* tacked lazily and swept up aft. Her cannon roared, and the *Aydah* was pushed sideways as her keel timbers gave way to that leaden onslaught.

119

Fletcher felt the ship dying under his bare feet.

She was settling fast, filling with water. The deck tilted sharply as the waves dragged her downward. Men pinned by broken bulkheads or fallen cannon were screaming in agony and fright, for the rest of the crew were leaving them behind in their haste to float the cockboats and man their thwarts. As the waves washed in over them, those men would gurgle and drown, held helpless.

It came to Fletcher that he would drown, too. The corsairs were riddled with panic. They could think only of their places in the tenders that were being dropped overboard in such haste. Even Mustafa reis forgot his vengeance in his hurry to save his skin. Fletcher expected to feel a pistol ball in his back at any moment, but it never came. One minute the *Aydah* was all confusion and rushing, yelling men; the next, it was silent as the sea into which it was being sucked so swiftly.

He fought the rope that held his arms around the mast. He flailed his body this way and that, but was anchored firmly. When the *Aydah* went down, he would go with it.

He did not see the lookout in the crow's nest of the *Constitution* take the spyglass from his eye, and shout down at Captain Stephen Decatur where he stood calm and relaxed in his blue uniform jacket and white breeches, his knee-high boots polished until they glittered. He could not hear the captain's orders as a small boat was swung outward and lowered swiftly to the waves. A dozen seamen scampered down the rope ladder and into the tender.

Then the cockboat was shooting across the green waves toward him. A lieutenant in the bow was kicking his feet free of his half-boots, preparatory to swinging up onto the partly submerged deck of the sinking corsair.

Salt water was swirling about the lieutenant's left ankle as his knife bit into the rope that held Fletcher. Gentle hands caught and lifted him; then he was being lowered between the thwarts, and the oars flashed as the small boat shot away from the dying *Aydah* like a frightened thing.

Fletcher stared up into the wind-reddened face of an officer whose eyes were warm with sympathy.

"American?" the lieutenant asked.

Fletcher nodded. "Lieutenant, United States Marines. Imprisoned at Tripoli. Escaped. Can tell your commander about fort's defenses. I—"

It was then that Fletcher fainted.

Fletcher opened his eyes in a berth deck cabin. He lay in a narrow bunk, facedown, his left cheek cradled on a mattress. All around him he could hear the sounds of a warship at sea: the faint voices of singing men working at the deckplanks with mops and pails, the peculiar metallic rasp of a cannon being cleaned, the steady chant of seamen heaving the log.

A seaman in striped jersey and wide white trousers came to his feet when he saw Fletcher staring at him. His grin was infectious.

"You be a lucky man, sir! Fortunate it was that one of the boys was sweepin' the pirate's deck with his glass."

Fletcher croaked, "Fortunate it was, seaman."

The sailor knuckled his brow. "I got orders to alert the captain when you come to, sir. If you'll be excusing me, I'll go abovedecks."

It seemed to Fletcher that he just had time to roll over on his side—even the weight of the thin sheets was intolerable on his lacerated back—when the door opened and the redfaced lieutenant whose knife had freed him from the mainmast of the *Aydah* pushed his head into the cabin.

"He looks fit and fine, Captain," he grinned, and stood aside.

Captain Stephen Decatur came into the room with brisk steps. He was a young man, only in his middle twenties in this spring of 1805. Like his fellow officers, Isaac Hull and Charles Stewart, he was building the foundations of naval greatness on the decks of the young American navy that was on blockade duty in the Mediterranean. Already he had distinguished himself by slipping into the harbor of Tripoli and burning the *Philadelphia* where her corsair captors had moored her, in February, 1804. While commanding the twelve-gun schooner *Enterprise,* he had served also as aide to Commodore Edward Preble before Barron replaced him.

Of middle height, he had dark curly hair and piercing eyes. The resolute energy that burned in his strong body revealed itself by his quick, catlike movements. His dark blue jacket was set with silver buttons and lace, and the

121

epaulettes at his shoulders were thick with gold. He dragged a chair toward him and sat down.

"Can you talk, lieutenant?"

"I think so, sir. Luckily, they'd just begun with the cat when your foredeck cannon spoke."

"The ship's doctor says you'll be on your feet in a day or thereabouts. Lieutenant Marley tells me you know the defenses of the Tripoline fort."

"I do, sir. But more important than that, there's the matter of a secret fleet Yussuf Caramanli is building. . . ."

Fletcher talked for almost an hour as Decatur sat tight-lipped, listening. When he was done, weakness washed across him in surging waves. His eyelids felt weighted with leaden sinkers. He scarcely felt the touch of the captain's fingers at his shoulder, nor heard the voice with which he ordered him back to sleep. He was snoring as the door closed behind the two officers.

In the companionway, Decatur said crisply, "Order on all sail, Lieutenant. We'll stand full and by, south by east for the Tripoline coast, to rendezvous with the fleet off Benghazi. After that, we'll go looking for these ships Yussuf Caramanli is building. When we find them—well, I think our little war will be a long way over."

"Yes, sir!" agreed the smiling lieutenant, and saluted briskly.

Fletcher was in uniform three days later, off Farawa Island. Once again the tight blue marine jacket, with its turnback skirts and rows of silver buttons, fitted his chest snugly. He stood at the rail with Lieutenant Marley as the *Constitution* skirted the low African coastline.

Some days before, Commodore John Rodgers had arrived from the United States in the *Congress* to replace Commodore Samuel Barron as commander of the Mediterranean fleet. Captain Stephen Decatur, commanding the *U.S.S. Constitution,* was given command of the *Congress* while the *Constitution* was made flagship of the squadron. In this late May of 1805, the United States Mediterranean fleet was at its peak of strength. The frigates *Constitution* and *Constellation, Congress* and *Essex,* the sixteen-gun brigs *Argus* and *Siren,* and the two twelve-gun schooners, built with shallow drafts for inshore work, the *Nautilus* and the *Vixen,* made it a formidable fighting force.

Now, with the *Constitution* showing the way, the other frigates came fast abeam, all sails flying, sunlight glinting on their cannon and copper rigging. Behind them, strung out astern, came the brigs and schooners. It was a fine spring morning, with the sun warming and the blue skies empty of clouds.

They had come up in the night, moving without lights. In the distance, the glimmer of lanterns and bonfires showed them where men worked feverishly against time to ready brigantines and feluccas for sea duty. All that night, from the dogwatch to the graveyard watch, men had slept at their battle stations, ready at the first blast of the boatswain's pipe to leap to action. Now they waited with the early morning sun on their backs, crouched near their gleaming cannon, ready and eager for the signal to touch matches to vents.

The pirates had seen them. Desperate men were running on the sands, striving with sweat and muscle to turn the twenty-four pounders, seeking to roll the cannons around to face the sea and the big ships that had materialized so miraculously out of the early dawn mists.

A voice roared on the *Constitution's* gundeck. An instant later, the cannons spat their flame and iron. In this first attack, chain shot—twin cannonballs linked with chains—was poured along the stretch of beach. Usually used against the rigging of an enemy ship, this screaming weight of linked iron cut a bloody swathe along those clean white sands. Men were ripped in half, or sheared of hands and legs by that rush of whirling metal. Gun crews went down as if beneath a giant flail.

The *Constitution* moved on, and now the *Constellation* poured its weight of shot across the beaches. Then it was the turn of the other ships, their crews eager and grim, their master gunners sighting and shouting out their orders. One after another, a dozen broadsides raked the bloodsoaked sands.

Now the *Constitution* was coming back, its port cannon ready.

Five swift brigantines, all the ships that the corsairs had outfitted for sea, came to meet the big frigate. The American ship slowed its advance, giving the *Congress* and the *Essex* time to join her. They closed on the five Tripolines together, outnumbered but confident.

123

Chain shot had been exchanged for solid iron. As the vessels closed, the starboard cannon of the *Constitution* exploded in a deafening outpouring of flame and metal. One of the brigantines reeled back under that solid onslaught, her timbers ripped and splintered. On the main deck, where the twenty-four pounders were, powder monkeys ran with round kegs. Half naked men worked at the cannons, swabbing them on the starboard side, and reloading the breeches on the port side. Officers moved back and forth, calling out orders calmly, as if they were doing no more than testing their marksmanship.

From the rigging, selected marines and sailors were pouring riflefire into the open decks of the nearest brigantine, dropping corsair after corsair at his battle station. Two hundred yards away, the *Argus* was slipping between two brigantines, both broadside batteries erupting simultaneously.

The *Constitution* moved on through the water. Now its port batteries were aiming at the fourth corsair ship. Now they were exploding.

Behind them, the *Congress* was closing with the last pirate vessel. Sailors and marines with bayonets fixed to their rifles, were shooting and running forward as the grapnels swung overhead. As the two ships bumped freeboards, the Americans brought their bayonets into play.

Lieutenant Marley was pointing aft, where the *Nautilus* and *Vixen* were swinging in line past the beaches, discharging chain shot in successive broadsides. "No man can live in that," he said grimly. "Inside an hour, there will be only dead men and smashed cannons left on those sands."

It was hard to talk and harder to listen in the crashing roar of the spar deck cannons. Fletcher merely nodded and caught hold of the starboard rail as the *Constitution* gave to another broadside. The smell of burned gunpowder and sweating men came to him in the wind. This was not his first action at sea, but the old excitement was still there, making his heart jump under his tightly buttoned service jacket. His hand itched to be around a pistol butt or a swordhilt, but his orders were to remain with Lieutenant Marley and observe the Tripoline fleet.

Two wounded brigantines were closing with the *Constitution*. If they could board and capture her, and turn her weight of cannon against her sister ships, they yet might salvage victory from this debacle. Fletcher watched their advance, saw the half naked fighting men crouched behind the gunwales, pistols and scimitars in their brown hands, saw grapnels being swung from the netted shrouds.

The *Constitution* bided its time until the corsairs were within twenty yards. Then their gun deck and spar deck cannon exploded. The brigantines were wreathed in white smoke, only their towering masts and slatting sails showing. Men screamed and moaned from the shelter of that smoke. Timbers splintered. Masts cracked and fell.

The American ship slid on, away from the broken corsairs.

As the wind caught the gunsmoke and blew it toward the shoreline, they could see the sinking Tripolines wallowing in the surging sea. Without masts and sails—one of the corsairs had lost its rudder in that iron hail—they floated helplessly. More than half their crews lay dead. Most of the others were wounded near to dying.

Commodore Rodgers, now commanding the *Constitution,* turned his attention to the *Essex,* where she was locked gunwale to gunwale with two pirate ships. The *Congress* was hurling broadside after broadside at the fifth and last pirate ship, which was settling rapidly by the stern.

The men on the *Essex* were fighting savagely. Their gun crews had abandoned their cannon, after one final broadside, for pistols and muskets. The pirates came to them in surging, screaming waves, maddened by battle lust. Their naked chests invited the thrust of steel, and the marines and seamen decimated their ranks with bayonet play.

The *Constitution* could not fire on the pirate ships for fear of hitting the *Essex,* but it could send a fresh wave of marines aboard one of the Tripolines. Under the stabbing impact of those bayonets, the pirates went down like tenpins on a village green. Freed of the necessity of meeting two foes, the crew of the *Essex* swung around to their port side, where the corsair crew was striving to come aboard.

But the fight was over, after that.

The single Tripoline brigantine that was still floating when the *Essex* cut loose her grapnels, was set afire and allowed to drift inshore with the tide. Those of the pirates still alive were taken in a tender to Farawa Island and put ashore. Then a landing party went in to spike what remained of the Tripoline cannons.

It may have been the fact that fighting had gone on

125

around him all day without his playing a part in it that made Fletcher so restless that night. Commodore Rodgers kept him away from the other men, ordering Lieutenant Marley to walk beside him whenever he took a stroll on the deck (as if he were a spy, he thought to himself). He grew morose as the *Constitution* lifted its anchor and put out to sea with the bloody beach a thin strip fast disappearing behind its aft rail.

Then he thought of Eve Doremus.

So much had happened to him since Shellah had come to his little dungeon cell that he had not thought of Eve, except when he was falling asleep, or in the dreams that had come to him while he lay in the little bunk as his back mended.

Now she was with him again. He relived that night in his tiny palace room, when they had first been together. In memory, he tasted her lips once more, and felt the warm smoothness of her skin against his own. Those days on the *Burak,* while Yussuf Caramanli lay between life and death with Marlani Chamiprak at his side lest he wake to find her gone, he and Eve had leaned together on the rail, facing into the wind and holding hands, or strained against each other for a kiss during a snatched moment, sheltered by the striped deck tent.

He wanted nothing so much as to see her again, and hold her in his arms. They had had little time for the whispered secrets and confidences that are so much a part of romance. Their kisses and caresses had to be hidden things, exchanged only when Marlani Chamiprak and the corsair crew were nowhere near them. Those starry nights when they had sat with their backs propped to the maindeck scuppers came back to him. In little murmurs they had talked of the house he would build, close by the family plantation in Virginia, where they would raise their children and entertain the neighbors.

Fletcher clenched his fists against the yearning inside him. He tried to force his thoughts away from the future, back to the present and to the fact that Eve Doremus was a prisoner of Yussuf pasha.

When the Americans attacked, she would be killed. Even if the *Constitution* and her companion ships did not sail past the Caramanli castello with broadsides blazing, she would still be killed in the market square. Mustafa reis had promised as much, before he strung Stephen Fletcher up to the shrouds. She would be tortured to death in the great square, the corsair captain had said, if Fletcher was not recaptured within the month.

Fletcher paled.

"Damnation," he whispered. "How long have I been gone from Tripoli?"

He found Lieutenant Marley belowdeck, in the wardroom. From his sea bag the lieutenant drew a battered, torn calendar. He said thoughtfully, scratching his jaw, "Let's see, now. We picked you up about three weeks ago. . . ."

"I was two days and two nights at sea by that time."

"Took a full week for you to recover from that lashing, and another week and a half to find the hidden fleet. I'd guess you've been aboard now almost a month!"

Almost a month! Then how long was left Eve Doremus to stay alive?

Fletcher went white. "Must see the commodore! No time to waste. Girl in Tripoli—"

Commodore Rodgers was polite, but adamant. He listened to the story Fletcher poured into his ears, sitting grim and rigid in his cabin, but he only smiled sympathetically and shook his head. "I'm sorry, Lieutenant. I can't give you permission to leave ship at this moment. We're sailing straight for Tripoli. You know its innermost defenses. You—"

"But, sir! I've drawn you a dozen maps of the castello and the walls, and what lies behind them!"

Rodgers smiled. "True enough, and I'm grateful. But I want you at my elbow as we begin our attack, Lieutenant. I'm sorry. I've only one course to follow. Permission must be refused."

The commodore turned to the papers littering the top of his desktop under the hanging glass lamp. He looked old and worried, with the lamplight painting black shadows around his eyes. Fletcher stared at him a moment longer, then came to his feet.

"Thank you anyhow, sir."

As Fletcher opened the door, the commodore lifted his head. "A moment, Lieutenant. A word of advice. The penalty for departing ship in the face of attack on an enemy post is death."

"I know, sir," replied Fletcher heavily, and closed the door behind him.

The *U.S.S. Constitution* and the *Constellation*, followed in single line by the *Congress* and *Essex* and the other ships of the fleet, swept past the low African shoreline midway between Jerba and Tripoli. Overhead the stars glittered like faint blue fires far away. The night was warm with approaching summer, and from somewhere forward there was the sound of sailors singing.

Fletcher eyed the low coastline eagerly.

He stood by the rail in complete uniform, the riding lanterns catching the polished leather of his tall service hat. If he could only swing overside and down into that water gurgling past the bulwarks! It wouldn't be a long swim. A little more than a mile perhaps, at this distance. Once he was ashore, it shouldn't be too hard to find a little coastal inn where a horse could be bought, or a Bedouin encampment—desert nomads on their way to Tripoli to trade—where fleet Arab barbs would be exchanged for a few of the silver that Fletcher had received for back pay.

Fletcher grimaced and turned from that intriguing shore. Death was the penalty for doing what he thought about, here in the May night. They shot you for desertion. If he went overside, and if by some miracle of fate, he could save Eve, he would die himself. If he stayed where he was like an obedient officer, Yussuf pasha would torture to death the woman he loved.

His fist clenched hard as the sweat came out on his face.

For three hours, Fletcher stood by the rail. He went back over his life, step by step, from the days when he played Captain Kidd in the Fletcher plantation manse, through his trips to the ironworks in Baltimore with his father, to his training days and his life as a marine officer on the *Adams* and the *Constellation* and the *Philadelphia*. Against all that and his hope for the future, he balanced a pretty Boston girl with black hair and very soft, white skin, named Eve Doremus.

The scales tilted sharply.

His eyes ran the length of the fighting deck of the big frigate. He studied the spar deck cannons thrust through the gun deck ports and the neat, trim look of their breeching tackle. The *Constitution* did not need him, not nearly as much as Eve Doremus needed him at this moment. There were sailors and marines aboard to do the fighting. The maps he had drawn for Commodore Rodgers were secure in his cabin locker. Stephen Fletcher would be as useful on the gundeck of this fighting ship as he had been when she and her sister ships had smashed Yussuf Caramanli's secret fleet at Jerba. All he had done then was watch; all he would do when the *Constitution* stood in against Tripoli was stand beside Lieutenant Marley and marvel at the gunnery magic of her cannon crews.

Stephen Fletcher smiled grimly. "It's simply a matter of my offering my life to save hers!"

He waited until he was certain that no one watched him. Then he slipped out of his service jacket and put it on the deck beside his hat. With one hand gripping the rail capping, he went overside and down toward the cold waters swirling below.

CHAPTER 12

It was market day in Tripoli. From the surrounding countryside, swaying camels laden down with bales of Persian carpets and muslins paraded leisurely past the desert gate. Tiny wooden carts drawn by tireless donkeys creaked endlessly over the cobbled streets. Dealers in henna leaves and snuff went on foot, hawking their wares from wicker baskets in singsong voices. A group of Bedouin riders cantered through the crowd, the red silk tassels of their horses' headstalls shaking rhythmically, their long burnooses rippling about them. Women walked like strange ghosts, completely swathed in black silk *haiks*.

Where the Street of Smiths gave off the clanging ring of hammers on anvils and the leathery sound of bellows blowing at the forgefires, a man reined in a little desert horse. He was dressed like a desert dweller, but beneath the sheltering folds of the cloak were tight white breeches and kneeboots. The rider paused, indecisive.

Stephen Fletcher had crawled ashore on a sandy beach thirty miles from Tripoli, a little after midnight. Within forty minutes of wading ashore, he had come upon a little fire, where a Bedouin family lay encamped. Tall dark piles showed the produce of a season awaiting the morning packing of the camel panniers. A few scrawny horses, native animals to judge from their boniness, cropped at the esparto grass.

A handful of his silver coins purchased a horse—the worst-looking one of the lot, Fletcher knew, but it was a horse—and a burnoose. The Bedouin, who knew that Fletcher was an infidel but that his silver was blessed by Allah, gave him directions on how to reach Tripoli by early afternoon. He rode all night and most of the following morning, through the red dawn and early coolness into a blazing noon sun.

Now he turned the little barb and toed it forward, walking it slowly between the blacksmith shops. His eyes studied each face, each body in the red reflections of the forgefires. A hammer bouncing with metallic clangor on a horseshoe filled his ears, then was replaced by the heavier thud of a chain kepi fastened to a pointed corsair helmet. Sudanese worked most of the smithies, big black men from the east African coast along the Red Sea; but here and there a man with lighter skin stood out. These paler men were the slaves bought in the great square by the owners of the blacksmith shops.

Somewhere among these open shops was Mark Avison, the blond New Englander. Fletcher knew he must find Mark first, before he dared move another step toward the Caramanli palace. As he pulled the barb aside to let three desert Tauregs trot their ponies past him, their black litham veils hiding all but their eyes, Fletcher saw the American.

Avison was stripped to the waist, the muscles in his torso bulging as he hefted a big sledge. Fletcher toed his pony forward, leaning down as if staring toward a bad leg. Then he swung to the ground and brought the barb forward by the rein.

"Can you fix the fore off hoof?" he asked. He added in a whisper, "Don't appear to know me, Mark!"

The New Englander squatted down and looked carefully at the hoof. "I think we can have it good as new in a little while." He went on, "Steve! We'd about given you up! We heard you were captured, but rumor had it you'd gotten away."

In hoarse whispers, with their heads together over the little barb's hoof, Fletcher told him of the escape Shellah had engineered, of his flight in the little cockboat, his capture by Mustafa reis and his lashing. When he spoke of the *Constitution* and his rescue, Avison chuckled hoarsely.

"I know the *Constitution*. Whoever built her must have

130

put iron in her sides. Those corsair cannon will never harm her!"

When he heard of the destruction of the secret Tripoline fleet and of the sea fight off the Jerban coast, Avison scarcely breathed. "By the Lord Harry," he whispered, "I'd have given a year of my life to be there!"

"Rodgers would have kept you idle, watching what went on. He'd think you too valuable to risk in a fight."

They were drawing curious eyes, so Fletcher hissed, "Gather the men for a break tonight. At the Cyrenaica Gate, at midnight. Bring what weapons you've managed to hide with Yuvaz' help. I'm headed for the castello, to get Eve and Shellah, and the horses Yuvaz promised."

Avison nodded. Noticing the slave master staring hard, he growled in surly fashion, "I hear you, I hear you, son of the desert wind! I'll have the horse ready when you get back! Shaitan, what a tongue on the man!"

Fletcher smothered a grin and moved out into the street, losing himself amid the men and women hurrying by on their errands. An overful waterskin in the hands of a passing waterboy almost splattered his burnoose, but he snatched his cloak aside and howled a flurry of Islamic curses at the cowering boy. With his cloak wrapped about his lower face and only his eyes showing, he was as much the Bedouin as any who traveled the great ridges of the Sahara dunes.

It was growing dusk when Fletcher came to the garden gate of the Caramanli palace. Soon now, unless the palace routine had been changed in his absence, Shellah would be coming through the early evening darkness, a ring of keys jingling in her hand, to fetch the sellers of sweetmeats in the outer court. The wooden door was unlatched. It opened and closed behind him, and he hid himself behind a growth of large cactus, only thick enough to shelter him from the most casual glances.

Shellah came at last, as the lanterns were being lit in the selamlik.

She froze to a standstill at his whisper. "Shellah, on your life and mine! No sound! It's Stefan, come back to take you and Eve out of this place."

The desert girl had quick wits. She knelt on one knee and fumbled at her slipper. "How? How?" she breathed.

"You're on your way to fetch the sweetmeats sellers? Bring them back along this same path. I'll slip in among

131

them as they go. Undo the dungeon key from your keyring now. Drop it on the soft dirt to one side of the path. Then meet me back here at the street gate within the hour."

"Allah steals my wits! I almost think it may work!"

"Quickly, Shellah. Quickly! We'll meet Mark at midnight."

Her dark eyes opened wide at that, and her breathing quickened. Then her slim brown fingers fumbled at the keyring and detached a large iron key. In an instant she was on her feet and moving away.

Fletcher waited a long time, until he was positive he would not be seen. Then he slipped from the shrubbery and snatched up the key. He hid it in the pocket of his breeches, then went back behind the spiked branches of the cactus plant until Shellah should bring the sweetmeats sellers through the gardens. They came before he was well settled, babbling among themselves, their plaited baskets covered with snowy cloths, heaped high with powdered figs and dates. As they were moving past his hiding place, Fletcher slipped out and walked behind them.

No one noticed him, or the fact that he carried no basket. Each man was intent on his own business, and had no time to spare for the tall, cloaked figure that followed so closely. When they were under the arched portico, Fletcher slid aside into the black shadows and watched them file after Shellah toward the entry door of the haremlik stairs.

Fletcher waited a long time, until he was positive he the iron latch of a grilled door and then he was in a narrow corridor, moving with sure strides toward the stair at the far end leading into the damp cellars of the palace. It was quiet here in the late spring night. He could hear only faintly the strumming of a stringed instrument and the soft voice of a singing slave girl.

When the cellar stones were under his feet, he saw the guards.

There were two of them—big brown Libyans from the oasis country, clad in loose trousers and helmets and chain-mail shirts. They carried long scimitars; Fletcher was unarmed.

They lounged on a wooden bench to one side of the large, iron-reinforced oak door that gave entrance to the dungeon cells. There was no way of coming on them unexpectedly. It was fight and kill now, or die.

132

Fletcher kicked off his boots.

He came on bare feet out of the shadows, silent and swift. The guards saw him loom up in the light from the iron wall cresset; then he was on them. He came in a flying leap, that caught them half rising from the bench and knocked them to the ground in a rolling jumble of flailing bodies. Fletcher had to work fast. One or two loud outcries, and his surprise would be gone, the entire castello alerted.

He drove a fist in a short arc to the side of the nearest jaw. The man stiffened under him. Fletcher dropped him and rolled free, turning as his feet hit the ground to launch himself at the second man.

Panther-fast, he hit the second guard just as the man opened his mouth for the yell that would bring his fellows down on this mad nasrany. The shock of that flying impact drove the guard over onto his back and then Fletcher was astride him, his big hands closing around the guard's throat. Bracing his feet on either side of the guard's hips, he lifted him by the neck and drove his head down against the stone floor of the corridor. There was a sharp thwack and the guard went limp.

It took only a moment to gag and bind them with their belts and strips of linen torn from their loose trousers. Fletcher carried them one at a time into the dungeon where he dropped them in separate cells. Snatching up a discarded scimitar he thrust it into a scabbard and buckled its belt about his waist. Then he locked the big oaken door and moved off through the damp, dark cellars.

"Eve, Eve!"

His low call echoed through the cells, but there was no answer. His heart thudding heavily with an unnamed fear, Fletcher walked on. Am I too late? he asked himself. Has Yussuf Caramanli killed her already, before the month is finished?

He was deep in the dungeons now. Only the faint radiance from a distant oil lamp on the stone wall brightened the blackness. Was she down here at all, even if she were alive? Perhaps the pasha had her a prisoner up above, in some secret room of the haremlik! If that were so, how could he ever get her out of this huge pile of stone and stucco?

"Eve, where are you? Eve? Eve!"

He fought down his fear, walking steadily along the narrow corridors between the cells. A strange sound came to his ears after a while and he listened, standing unmoving, silent. A woman was sobbing, somewhere near here.

"Eve!"

His cry reverberated between the cells. After a moment he heard a whimpered, "Stephen? Stephen, is that really your voice? Or have I gone mad, down here all this time?"

He found her crouched on one hip before the bars of a cell. Her hands clung to the thick iron bars as she raised her tear-streaked face. "Is it you? Or am I seeing visions?"

His master key unlocked the cell and then she was in his arms, straining against him, shuddering and crying wildly. He let her sob herself out, kissing her silky, fragrant hair, enjoying the soft pressure of her body against his.

"Shellah will be waiting at the gate for us, dearest," he told her. "We're late now. We've no time to waste."

As they ran along the dungeon corridors, he told her bits of his adventures since the night of his arrest. Besides Shellah, he explained, Mark Avison and the others off the *Philadelphia*—those of them who were slaves and not being held for ransom—were gathering this night. Swords and horses would be waiting for them, close by the Cyrenaica Gate.

In exchange, she told him the only news in the castello. Marlani Chamiprak had been returned to the good graces of the pasha. Her story—that she had gone to Stephen Fletcher's little room to ask Eve Doremus to go to the haremlik and stitch on cushions, and that while Eve had gone on ahead, Stephen Fletcher had pulled Marlani back and tried to make love to her—won over Yussuf. Fletcher wondered idly what inducements the coppery desert woman had added to her arguments to convince her lord and master of her innocence. He chuckled wryly, but this was no time for guessing games. Shellah would be at the gate, and at the other end of the city, Mark Avison and the American slaves were waiting.

The night was dark and moonless. They came out of the haremlik portico to find Shellah crouched in the shadow of a pillar, trembling. "Mashallah!" she breathed, running to Eve and clasping her in her brown arms. "I'd given you both up for dead!"

Side by side, they ran for the garden gate.

Just as Fletcher was stretching out his hand for the latch-pull, the oaken door opened. Two men stood there, blocking

134

their way. One was Yuvaz the Armless, crouched forward, shaking wildly in terror, his mouth dripping blood where he had been struck, again and again.

The other man was Mustafa reis.

Shellah cried out in dismay. Eve gasped and whirled as if to plead with Fletcher. Only the big marine kept his head. He lunged forward, hitting the corsair sea captain, sending him reeling backward, out into the street. Fletcher was after him in a moment, dragging the scimitar from his belt.

Mustafa reis bellowed his triumph.

"Nasrany dog, son of a dog and brother of dogs! You've played into my hands! No man in Tripoli is my match with cold steel. I'll carve your face and put out your eyes, but I won't kill you. I'll let Yussuf pasha have that pleasure!"

His steel came flashing down, a faint white blur in the dark night. Fletcher met it with his own, felt the shock of the contact run up into his arm and shoulder. The corsair feinted and slashed sideways at Fletcher's hip. The American went backward, barely turning the stroke.

The clash of steel blades would bring the castello guards on the double. They would flood the streets with men and block every exit. Burdened with two women, Fletcher would never make the Cyrenaica Gate before his capture. Everything he planned had gone wrong! Everything for which he had sacrificed his standing as a marine officer, for which he had taken the lead-tipped cat on board the *Aydah,* was gone up in smoke!

Suspecting the American's despair, Mustafa reis began to gloat at him. "Infidel pig! Did you think to fool the children of Allah? I found this armless thing visiting with his friends tonight. I followed him like his own shadow. I know now what sort of traitor he is! When my tongue makes a present of you to my pasha, it will also offer him Yuvaz. Hai! The birds will have good eating shortly! The two of you, perched on the torture scaffold, with your women beside you!"

Sweat ran down Fletcher's face, blinding him. Never before had he faced a sword like this, that seemed to be everywhere at once. It cut down from overhead and sliced at him sideways and came thrusting up less than a foot from the street stones. He skipped and danced, flailing this way and that with his blade, knowing inside him that it would be

135

only a matter of seconds before that keen edge was slicing at his cheek.

"Yuvaz," he gasped. "Take the women—Shellah and Eve! Run for the Cyrenaica Gate. I'll hold Mustafa reis until you're safely away!"

The corsair captain shouted now as he wove in with his scimitar, stamping heavily to the attack. "Ho, the castaello! Ho, the guards! To me! To me!" His blade sliced sideways suddenly, out of an overhead molinello, and Fletcher felt the sharp, hot bite of steel along his forearm.

Feet were pounding along the garden paths, behind the high palace wall.

"Run, man!" he shouted at the trembling Yuvaz. "If you hope to save your own neck, get the women out of here!"

Yuvaz uttered a wet, choking cry. Then he was running soundlessly, with Eve Doremus and Shellah at his heels. As Fletcher thrust into a savage attack at the corsair captain, their pounding feet faded into silence.

Mustafa reis laughed harshly. "You stupid fool! Do you think you can get out of Tripoli? When his guards tell Yussuf Caramanli what's been going on tonight, he'll have every man in the palace after you!"

As if he had hoped to distract Fletcher with his words, the corsair captain swept in with whirling blade. Fletcher was blinded for a moment, so that he fought purely by instinct, guarding himself in tierce and prime. The steel blades grated, fell away to meet again, clanging savagely. Too late, Fletcher realized that Mustafa reis was making him turn as he fought, to swing about so that his back was to the closed gate in the garden wall. When the castello guards swarmed out, they would have him at their mercy.

Desperately, he fought to free himself from that intolerable position. His arm swept his curving blade this way and that, but Mustafa reis held like a rock, fighting only on the defensive. Behind him, Fletcher heard hoarse voices raised in excited query, heard the latch grate as it lifted.

For one moment, the corsair captain took his eyes from the American to look past him at the opening door.

In that instant, Fletcher hurled himself forward, his blade held straight before his lunging body. Like that, the scimitar went into Mustafa's belly, the point protruding out his back by a foot of bloody steel.

Fletcher did not wait for him to fall. In one bound he

was past him, wrenching the dying man's sword from his nerveless fingers. On bare feet he was running faster than he had ever run, down the dark street, leaving the guards bending over the sea captain whose body was even now jerking convulsively in his death agonies.

"Yussuf himself will ride out tonight to find us! He'll search the palace and find the two guards I left tied in the dungeons. He'll learn Eve and Shellah are gone, together with Yuvaz, and will smell out the rest by instinct!"

Five of the guards were coming after him.

Fletcher tried to lose them. He ran easily, turning down an alley where its mouth loomed black and inviting. He went up a garden wall, ran across the flaggings and took the far wall in a single leap. He found narrow little pathways between the steep sides of buildings. As he ran, he went as nearly as he could in an easterly direction, toward the escape gate where the American slaves would be waiting for him.

He had no way of knowing whether Yuvaz and the girls would win free. More than once he paused to listen for their footfalls, but only an occasional drunken voice or the soft splashing of fountain waters answered his listening ears. Faintly in the distance, he heard the shouts of the castello guards as they hunted him.

Now, as he ran, he angled his course more directly toward the Cyrenaica Gate. If anyone knew the shortcuts that would take Eve Doremus and Shellah to the waiting American, Yuvaz would know them. He put worry from his mind, and stretched his legs for speed.

He saw the horses first, saddled and bridled, in little clusters close by the shop awnings, where the sellers of waterskins and camel saddles gathered in the daytime to hawk their wares. The wooden gate was closed, but a man leaned in its shadows, a naked scimitar in his hand. As Fletcher came pounding up, the solitary guard moved forward. In the dim light Fletcher recognized Caleb Framingham.

"Steve?"

"Yussuf himself is hunting us in the streets. I just killed Mustafa reis. What about Eve? Did she—?"

A soft cry was his answer. Fletcher whirled to take Eve Doremus against him as she hurtled out of the black shadows of a saddlemaker's awning.

137

"If you'd been killed back there—oh, I didn't want to run and leave you! I would die! Darling, darling! Oh, Steve—sweetheart—"

He folded her in his arms and kissed her. The embrace lasted only a brief moment before Mark Avison, Ned Brunner and the others were around them, whispering fiercely.

"Steve, come on!"

"No time for that, man!"

They could hear the outcries of the palace soldiers as they came running up the Street of the Winesellers, which lead at right angles into the gate square. In a moment it would be touch and go. By the time Caleb Framingham and the two men working with him on the huge crossbar of the wooden gate could open those ponderous doors, the palace guards would be on them. Their pounding feet echoed louder every passing moment.

Fletcher gripped Mark Avison by a wrist. "Get into the shadows, Mark. All of you but Yuvaz, Eve and Shellah! We'll let them see us at the gate."

"What about us, Steve?"

"Hide in the awning shadows! They'll be so busy looking at us, they won't see you, until you hit them."

Avison chuckled. His curly yellow hair was like a halo on his head in the faint radiance of the houselamp as he swung it, crying out softly, "You men, into the shadows. Steve's going to bait a trap for them."

Chuckles and mutterings of approval sounded a moment as the men disappeared under the awnings and into the deeply recessed doorways of the adjacent houses. For nineteen months, they had been slaves to the Tripolines. They had eaten rotten food and drunk stale water. The backs of some of them bore livid red scars where a lash had flailed them. All were gaunt and lean and vengeful. It hurt their spirit to run from Tripoli without a chance to hit back at their former masters. Now that chance was being given them.

In the shadows, hands worked convulsively on the grips of Moslem scimitars or tightened angrily around the curving butts of longbarreled Turkish pistols. Bright eyes watched Fletcher and the armless man with the two girls as they ran for the big wooden gate, saw them struggle frantically with the crossbar. The horses were out of sight, hidden by a garden wall.

138

The trap was set, the bait was ready.

The guards came in a shouting, running mass of waving swords and clanking mail shirts. They filled the streets from building wall to building wall. And towering high above them all was Yussuf Caramanli, on an Egyptian stallion. At sight of· Fletcher, who whirled and stood with his back to the oaken doors, he howled in triumph.

"Take them alive. All four of them! The man who harms them dies in their place!"

The janissaries were blind to everything but the two girls and the man. Yuvaz they discounted: what harm could a man without arms do to a castello guard? The girls they ignored with the inborn arrogance of the Oriental male. They came for Fletcher, round shields up and scimitars poised to ward off his blows.

The foremost of them was within a dozen feet of the Cyrenaica Gate when Mark Avison brought his waiting Americans out of the awning shadows. On the opposite side of the cobbled street, from the recessed doorways of shops and private buildings, Caleb Framingham and Ned Brunner led their fellows. From left and right the Americans hit the palace guards.

The street was filled with dead and dying Tripolines at that first exchange of swordcuts. The Americans struck with speed and savagery. This was their chance to pay for starved bellies and whipped backs, manacle-scarred wrists and ankles, and all the scorn and contempt they had been forced to swallow for months. The guards could not stand to them. Scimitars were beaten aside; unprotected necks were slashed where helmets and chain-mail could not protect them; clawing hands seized shields and yanked them down.

Yussuf Caramanli bellowed like a wounded bull. He ripped out his own blade, but the bodies that pressed around him terrified his horse and almost unseated him. His eyes bulged from his head, for wherever he looked he saw Americans: angry, vengeful, fighting like the archdemons of Shaitan. Their swords were blurred streaks of silvery lightning. Their faces were dark and angry and very terrifying, like remembered nightmares come to life.

"Tumar, Tumar!" he cried. "To me, to me! These infidel pigs will kill me! Surround me!"

But the captain of his guard was too busy with Stephen Fletcher to hear him. With his breath rasping in his throat, with blood running from his arm and thigh where the Americano's scimitar had cut—*Bi'llah!* how the man could wield that thing! He was in no condition to worry about anyone's safety but his own. Slowly, Tumar fell back until he was pressed into another guard who fought for his very life on the gatesquare cobblestones. Tumar saw the scimitar coming at his head and lifted his blade. Too late, he realized the molinello was but a feint, and that Fletcher's real target was his unprotected right side. The next moment the cold steel was biting deep into his flesh and he was stumbling, dying as he crumpled.

Although Tumar did not hear the pasha's cry, Yuvaz the Armless did. He sidled away from the gate, running in his lurching way, grinning wolfishly. He skirted the rim of the struggling men, dancing a little in his intentness. If only he had an arm with a sword in it!

Fletcher leaped over the body of the dying captain, his scimitar blade a flail before him, slicing a path for himself through the packed castello guards. The sight of Yussuf Caramanli put a ferment in his blood. Suddenly Stephen Fletcher had plans for the pasha of Tripoli. Savagely, he fought to reach him.

A twisted knot of struggling men lurched into Fletcher and sent him spinning sideways. Fighting to recover balance, he fell to his knee. An open space cleared around him, as if by magic. Looking up, he saw Yussuf Caramanli spurring his stallion forward. High over his head the royal scimitar moved, for a moment. Then it was coming down, straight at Fletcher's unprotected head.

Yuvaz the Armless came out of nowhere, lifting himself with all his strength in a wild leap, hitting hard against Yussuf.

The pasha screamed as he felt himself falling. His feet slid out of the ivory stirrups and the cobbles came rushing up to meet him. He landed heavily and lay there, paralysed for a moment.

Yuvaz threw himself at him, mouth gaping open. Like a starving animal he buried his teeth in Yussuf Caramanli's throat, and bit down hard.

The pasha screamed thickly, his fingers sinking into Yuvaz' shoulders. The thick body convulsed in agony, whipping the lighter man sideways. But Yuvaz kept his jaws tightly clenched on that fat throat as the two men rolled across the square, struggling silently.

When his throat seemed about to explode, Yussuf re-membered the curving dagger in his sash. His fingers fumbled for it, closed around the haft. An instant later the slim length of the dagger was buried in the armless man's chest.

Yuvaz fell free, lungs heaving wildly.

Fletcher caught the pasha's hand, twisting it at the wrist. The curved dagger went flying. Then Fletcher was turning the pasha face down on the cobbles, whipping his sash loose, kneeling on the small of his back and bringing both wrists up behind him. He tied the sash tightly about those wrists, tied and knotted it, and then stood up.

Death was blurring Yuvaz' eyes as Fletcher knelt beside him.

"I die happy, nasrany," the armless man said. "You will take Yussuf as your prisoner to your American ships. They will hang him from a yardarm, and Hamet will be pasha once again in Tripoli."

"Yussuf is my prisoner. I will take him to the American ships. It will be as you say."

Yuvaz jerked heavily. His breath grew labored and hoarse. Slowly, his head shook from side to side. "Allah is waiting for me. Allah and the gardens of delight. I will have arms in paradise, nasrany. Arms and a whole body, and there will be houris to delight my every waking hour. . . ."

His eyes open wide, Yuvaz laughed. And then he died.

Fletcher stood up. The castello guards were fleeing down the side streets. Only the Americans and the fallen pasha were left in the square. Fletcher pushed his scimitar back into its scabbard and bending over Yussuf, lifted him to his feet.

The sailors and marines crowded around, exclaiming in their delight. One or two wanted to butcher him instantly and leave his blood staining the stones that their own blood had stained, but Fletcher was adamant about his prisoner's disposal.

"Capturing Yussuf changes everything," he told them. "We don't need to go horseback riding for seven hundred miles. We'll borrow the fishing smacks on the beach and go out to find the *Constitution* and the rest of the squadron. Having the pasha of Tripoli as our prisoner means the Barbary war is over!"

They howled their approval, and eager hands went to

141

work on the crossbar of the Cyrenaica Gate.

As Fletcher followed them, walking hand in hand with Eve, a little behind the silent Yussuf Caramanli, he remembered suddenly that he was a deserter.

When he set foot on the deck planks of the *Constitution*, Commodore John Rodgers would hang him from the bowsprit.

CHAPTER 13

Fletcher never knew whether it was shock or amusement that glinted in the eyes of Commodore Rodgers as he stared at the pasha of Tripoli standing so meekly before his desk in the captain's cabin. The American commander cleared his throat and looked from Fletcher to Eve Doremus and the pasha. Then he stared at Shellah and Mark Avison.

"Yussuf Caramanli himself," he said at last, and hit the desk top with a palm.

They had come aboard the *Constitution* in the early morning hours, while a mist still hung over the Mediterranean. As the entire fleet hove to, and the commanders of the *Congress* and the *Essex* came flying across the water in cockboats, the freed American slaves were welcomed on the frigate's spar deck with shouts and laughter, with much clapping of backs and shaking of hands. A grinning lieutenant took Fletcher and Avison, with the pasha and the girls at their heels, to meet the commodore.

"Well," said Rodgers. "Well!"

Then he scowled and glanced sideways at Fletcher. "I have some recollection of forbidding you to leave ship, sir! This is desertion!"

Fletcher paled. Beside him, Eve Doremus gasped and stepped forward. It may have been the light in her angry eyes, or the words that he anticipated from her trembling lips, but the commodore hastily raised a hand.

"However, I am sure there is no written record of my order, and equally as sure that I can easily forget what was said between us. Lieutenant Fletcher, my heartiest congratulations!"

Rodgers came to his feet and walked around the edge of his desk with outstretched hand. He was introduced to Eve

142

Doremus and to Shellah, and then he swung on Yussuf Caramanli.

"Well, sir! Fate and a marine lieutenant have put you in my hands. The choice for peace or war is up to you. Shall I go on with my intended assault on your city, hanging you from the bowsprit to discourage opposition? Or shall we make peace between our countries?"

There was no hesitation in Yussuf Caramanli. His brother Hamet was at Derna with General Eaton. If he swung with a noose about his neck from the bowsprit of the *Constitution*, Hamet would be pasha in his place. Surrender was a bitter pill in his mouth, but it was sweeter than the loss of his pashaship and death by hanging.

"Peace," he croaked hoarsely. "Let there be peace forever between us!"

The Mediterranean night was warm and fragrant. At the quarterdeck rail of the *U.S.S. Constitution*, Eve Doremus leaned against her husband. The sky overhead was spangled with stars, and they could hear faintly the sound of strumming guitars. They had been married that afternoon, standing beside Shellah and Mark Avison, just before Commodore Rodgers had closeted himself with the pasha in his cabin to discuss the terms of surrender.

There were details to be ironed out that would require many visits from the pasha and his advisers to Commodore John Rodgers and Colonel Tobias Lear, consul general for Algiers, but those were matters that did not concern Eve Doremus. The anger of William Eaton at the easy treaty that would be made with the pasha of Tripoli, the abandonment of Hamet Caramanli to Yussuf's vengeance, were affairs for other heads than hers. At the moment all she was concerned about was this fine new husband she had so recently acquired.

At the moment he was saying, "I've made application for sick leave, darling. We'll spend our honeymoon in Virginia, at the manse."

"Sick leave," she giggled, leaning more heavily against him. "You seem uncommonly healthy to me at the moment, sir!"

His arms tightened, as he pulled her close. "Nevertheless, madam, I feel a weakness coming on. I fear only a visit to

143

our little cabin below decks, that the Commodore was good enough to assign us, can cure me of it."

Eve made a derogatory sound, then suddenly strained against him, feeling her heart flip over as their lips met in a long kiss that was at once an assurance of the magic of their love and a promise of rapture and fulfillment in the bright, serene days that lay endlessly ahead of them.

THE END